MFA

Writing Program at Vermont College

Intensive 11-Day residencies
July and January on the beautiful Vermont campus.
Workshops, classes, readings, conferences, followed by
Non-Resident 6-Month Writing Projects
in poetry and fiction individually designed during
residency. In-depth criticism of manuscripts.
Sustained dialogue with faculty.

Post-graduate Writing Semester
for those who have already finished a graduate degree
with a concentration in creative writing.

Scholarships and financial aid available.

For more information:
Roger Weingarten, MFA Writing Program, Box 772, Vermont College of
Norwich University, Montpelier, VT 05602 802–828–8840

Low-residency B.A. and M.A. programs also available.

Phyllis Barber
Francois Camoin
Mark Cox
Deborah Digges
Mark Doty
Jonathan Holden
Lynda Hull
Richard Jackson
Sydney Lea
Diane Lefer
Ellen Lesser
Susan Mitchell
Jack Myers
Sena Jeter Naslund
Christopher Noel
Pamela Painter
Frankie Paino
David Rivard
Gladys Swan
Sharon Sheehe Stark
Leslie Ullman
Roger Weingarten
W.D. Wetherell
David Wojahn

Visiting Writers include:
Julia Alvarez
Richard Howard
Brett Lott
Naomi Shihab Nye

WIN A RESTAURANT, MOTEL AND COUNTRY ESTATE
valued over $500,000
A WRITER'S DREAM

The Visconti's are moving to Florida. Their
country estate includes a 13-room home on 57
hillside acres with panoramic mountain view.
This and an established seafood restaurant and
motel located on Route 4 in Livermore, Maine
will be given away to the writer with the best
200 word essay on "Why I would like to operate Visconti's Country Lodge and Restaurant and
live in a country estate home."

The entry fee of $100 will be held in an escrow account according to the policy of the Attorney
General. All essays must be received by the March 31, 1994 deadline. Or **enter now** and a

bonus of a 1986 GMC Suburban 4×4 with
snow plow will be given to the winning entry
postmarked before December 31, 1993.

For a free copy of rules and more detailed
information send SASE: Visconti's Country
Lodge, P.O. Box 672, Livermore, Maine 04253
207/897-6729.

STORY

CONTENTS

STORY

ESTABLISHED 1931

FOUNDING EDITORS
Whit Burnett and Martha Foley

EDITOR
Lois Rosenthal

MANAGING EDITOR
Paul Mandelbaum

ASSISTANT EDITORS
Laurie Henry, Catherine White

ADMINISTRATIVE MANAGER
Rose Thiemann

EDITORIAL ASSISTANT
Joyce Miller

EDITORIAL BOARD
Will Blythe, Jane Ciabattari,
Alane Mason, Max Steele, Alice K. Turner

ART DIRECTOR
Clare Finney

COVER ARTIST
R.O. Blechman

PUBLISHER
Richard Rosenthal

CIRCULATION
David B. Lee

PRODUCTION
Barbara Schmitz, Director
Jane Garry, Production Manager

ADVERTISING SALES MANAGER
Joan Bambeck

Story (ISSN 1045-0831) is published quarterly by F&W Publications, Inc. **Editorial and Advertising offices** are located at 1507 Dana Avenue, Cincinnati, OH 45207; tel: 513-531-2222. Unsolicited manuscripts should include a self-addressed, stamped envelope (SASE); otherwise we cannot respond. Single copies: $5.95 plus $2.40 for postage and handling. Subscription rates: one year $22; two years $42; three years $60. Canadian and foreign subscribers add $7.00 per year surface mail, or $23.00 per year air mail, and remit in U.S. funds. GST R122594716. **Send all subscriptions, orders, and address changes to:** Story, P.O. Box 5068, Harlan IA 51593; tel: 1-800-888-0828. Available on microfiche, microfilm and 16mm from University Microfilms, Ann Arbor, Michigan 48106. Story is indexed in *Access* and *American Humanities Index*. Copyright 1990 by Story. Story is the trademark of F&W Publications, Inc. U.S.A. Newsstand Distribution by Eastern News Distributors, Inc., 2020 Superior St., Sandusky OH 44870. Second-class postage paid at Cincinnati OH, and additional mailing offices. **Postmaster: Send all address changes to Story, P.O. Box 5068, Harlan IA 51593.** Vol. 42 No. 1.

Printed in the United States of America.

STORY is printed on recycled paper.

The ecstasy of first love. A fan's passion for baseball. Devotion to the six o'clock news. The loyalty of a German shepherd. A romance with the mountains. The bond between brothers. An obsession with chocolate. All these loves (and more) qualify in STORY's 1994 Love Story Competition.

When writers crisscross the country, they frequently call when they hit Cincinnati. "Come for lunch," I say. "We'll have a picnic at the office. I'd love to show you STORY's home."

They stand in our lobby, amazed. "I pictured you in a musty old townhouse filled with boxes of manuscripts," they usually say. "What *is* this place? How did you wind up here?"

"Here" is a former Coca-Cola bottling works built in 1938. A gracefully curved Art Deco design—cutting edge for that era—the building was a showplace for years until changes in ownership left it in disrepair. F&W Publications (STORY's parent) purchased the building in 1986 and began a massive restoration that included removing paint from glass block, refurbishing six-inch thick, geometrically patterned, terrazzo tile floors, remilling huge stainless steel doors, and all sorts of other painstaking work to transform the bottling plant into a publishing house without infringing on the integrity of the structure. We were rewarded by being included on the National Register of Historic Places.

Phone when you're in town. I'll be glad to take you around.

• • •

I've been looking for years for a great Christmas story to run in our Winter issue. Then along came two. So you will find in this number Charles D'Ambrosio's "A Christmas Card," a story of loneliness when a love affair has ended during the holidays, and Susan Jane Gillman's lively take on a children's Christmas party at a transcendental meditation center in "Children with Mantras." Happy holidays.

• • •

We're inaugurating our Love Story Competition to search for stories of fondness and passion, tenderness and devotion, adoration and rapture. So whether you write of the ecstasy of first love, an obsession with chocolate, or the bond between brothers, seduce us with your most creative effort. Details are on pages 6 and 7.

— *Lois Rosenthal*

Where People Know Me

Late at night, long after the other residents in the senior care facility have gone to sleep, Big Grandma is wakeful. She whirs down the fourth floor hall in her electric wheelchair, past the nurses' station where the RN on duty is bent over a stack of medical records, and stops in front of the elevator. By the time security catches up with her, she is on the ground floor, headed out the lobby toward the parking lot. When they ask where she is going, she answers in Japanese, "Where people know me."

This is what the night nurse reports to my mother's oldest sister, Tee, who tells Mother, who calls long distance from Honolulu to tell me. Meanwhile, Aunt Tee has gotten in touch with Aunt Esther, the second oldest. Esther is offended at not being notified before my mother, even though Esther hasn't spoken to Big Grandma in years. Esther then gets back to Tee's daughter, who tells her mother, who phones my mother again and claims the whole thing is making it so she can't sleep nights. "You're the one who went to college," Aunt Tee says. "Why is Mama doing this to me?"

Here in Wyoming, Michigan, we've been having a week of record cold when Mother's call comes. The day's high was ten degrees, and the mercury's dropping as darkness falls. "You probably don't get many attempted escapes from the Senior Home there," she observes.

It's been more than ten years since my husband's search for a college teaching position took us away from the Islands; for the last four, we've lived in Michigan. During this whole time, between occasional visits, Mother and I have kept in touch several times a week by telephone. Recently I began my own business, freelancing from home as a technical writer, and she worries that I do not get out enough.

"There are too many hermits in this family," she says, right after telling me about the furor over my grandmother.

"Hermits? In *this* family?" I do not try to conceal my disbelief.

Today Dad has gone to a meeting of his retirees union, and she has the house to herself. "Days of Our Lives" is playing on the television in the background. After the family news, she gives me the rundown on her Birthday Girls Lunch Club, her arthritis exercise group, and her General Electric cooking class. The cooking class, which has adopted the motto "Encounter the good tastes of American cuisine," has moved on from ethnic desserts to ethnic salads. I am relieved to hear this since my waistline cannot tolerate many more encounters with the good tastes of Turkish baklava or Hungarian chocolate rum torte, which have been arriving with regularity by two-day priority mail.

It is hard to believe, laughing with her, that not long ago she had cancer surgery. But the doctors found the tumor early, and after a few months of recuperation, Mother has resumed her full social calendar. "It's like calling the sickness back to keep talking about it," she finally tells me, exasperated with being cross-examined about her latest medical checkup.

Now, before going off to prepare one of her ethnic desserts for a house-warming party, she fills me in on the neighborhood gossip. The Kanaheles' divorced son has moved back in with them. The Satos are traveling in India. The ugly Labrador retriever puppy next door has turned out to be a rottweiler. "I realize you're very busy . . . ," she segues, and I know that some-one will require birthday greetings, congratulations, or get-well wishes that *she* knows I will probably fail to send.

After we hang up, I sit in my darkening kitchen and watch the lights come on in the surrounding houses. It occurs to me that it's been days since I've seen any of the people who live in them.

The next time we talk, I tell her, "It's just that everyone around here keeps to themselves. Not like it is back home with everybody in each other's business. I can't hear myself think when I'm at home."

"I bet you get a lot of thinking done there." Her reply is without irony. "What do you think about?"

I can't help laughing then. "Oh, about what it's like back home."

My next visit to the Islands is in April, a few months after Big Grandma's near-escape. It's been a whole year since the last time I was back, when Mother was in the hospital. As soon as we arrive home from the airport, she starts reminding me to call people. "Don't forget to get in touch with Aunt Tee," she says. "And Aunt Esther—you know how she is. And your dad's sister Winnie has been phoning every day for a week. . . ."

It is late afternoon, and the humidity suddenly seems stifling. I go to the telephone and dial. When my husband, Hal, answers, there is an echo on the line. "Hello—hello." His voice fades in and out. "It's snowing—snowing—here. . . ."

The following morning, Mother and I drop by Esther's on our way to pick up Aunt Tee, who is going with us to visit Big Grandma. After her husband died a few years ago, Aunt Esther developed a fear of prowlers. She keeps all her windows fastened and her curtains drawn, even during the day. From the outside, it is impossible to tell that anyone is home, but Mother assures me that Esther hardly ever ventures out, unless accompanied either by herself or Tee. Aunt Esther has also had a locksmith install a dead bolt and a couple of additional locks on the living room door, and we can hear her undoing these as we stand on the front stoop, in the drizzle, with our cardboard boxes of homemade food.

After she lets us in, she disappears into the kitchen with the boxes, while we make our way through the stacks of newspapers and magazines lining the dim foyer, to the cluttered living room. A reading lamp glows on the end table next to the couch and a game show is playing on TV.

"Oh, 'Hollywood Squares,' " Mother says. "I watch that sometimes."

"I never do. I just keep the sound on for the company." Aunt Esther has materialized in the doorway. Her gaunt face is framed by stiff gray curls, and she is wearing a pants outfit of bluish gray.

When we leave, we invite her to come with us, but she declines, as she always does. "You were the favorite," she tells my mother. "Mama would never know that I was there."

The senior care facility occupies an entire wing of the medical center where Mother had her cancer operation the year before. As she, Aunt Tee, and I step out of the elevator, my aunt explains that the night staff have tried using medication, even physical restraint, to curtail Big Grandma's nocturnal wandering. But she has not let up on her determined resistance, which now includes occasional episodes of biting. "They have confiscated her dentures," Aunt Tee says, barely able to contain her mortification. If you bring any edibles for Big Grandma, you must go to the nurses' station and ask for her teeth. My aunt stops there to do so, and also to drop off the loaves of mango bread she has baked that morning. "Penance food," my mother whispers, as Aunt Tee distributes mango bread and expresses our thanks and apologies all around.

Big Grandma is sitting up in bed, dozing or pretending to doze, when we arrive at her room. Someone has dressed her in a baby-blue duster, trimmed with lace, and braided her white hair with pink and yellow ribbons. It is a new look for my ninety-six-year-old grandmother.

"Isn't that nice?" Aunt Tee says too brightly.

"Easter-egg colors," my mother adds. They both have the same fixed smile on their faces—the same smile, I suddenly realize, that is on mine. As we stand grimacing at Big Grandma, I resist the impulse to reach over and pull the ribbons from her hair.

She opens her eyes and lies back on the pillows, looking us over. Seeing that she has awakened, Mother gestures at me to approach, then says, "Look, look who's come to see you all the way from Michigan."

Big Grandma regards me blankly.

"It's Aya," my mother says. "From Michigan."

"Where?" Big Grandma asks, turning her good ear toward us.

"Mee-shee-gen," Mother repeats, louder.

"Ah," Big Grandma replies. She glances around the room, then back at me, comprehension dawning on her face. "I was wondering where this was."

In my memory, she is always dressed in dark colors, muted pin stripes and floral prints. She wears black *tabis* and straw slippers on her feet. Her hair is neatly oiled and pulled away from her face into a knot that is held in place with brown plastic combs. My grandmother seems always to have thought of herself as old. "You can't be free until you're old," she told me once. Though widowed young, she was never tempted to remarry. "I'd already had one husband," she said. "I didn't need another."

It seemed curious that she should speak of freedom with such spirit when she had more rules than anyone I ever knew. She had rules for what colors and styles to wear, rules for the order in which family members took a bath or got served dinner, and rules for eating at table (take less than your fill, never leave a single grain of rice in your bowl, refuse the last piece of chicken). The whole time she was living with Aunt Tee, for as far back as anyone could remember, the entire household was run by Big Grandma's rules.

There is a right way and a wrong way, according to Big Grandma. This is the right way to address an elder. This is how you speak to someone younger. This is how you sit. This is how you hold a cup. This is how you hand an object to another person. When I was six or seven, she instructed me in the proper use of chopsticks. After demonstrating how to hold them (thumb on the bottom, middle finger between, index finger on top), she handed me the pair and a bowl of Rice Krispies, then told me to pick out the grains of cereal, one by one.

My mother and her sisters also went through this training. "You had it easy," Aunt Tee assures me. "The only teaching aid she used with us was the flat side of a wooden cooking spoon."

After their father died and Big Grandma went to work as a live-in house-keeper for a wealthy family, she was away from home for days at a time. This left Aunt Tee, who was just twelve, at the head of a household of little girls.

"When you think about it, we could have gone wild," my mother says.

Then Aunt Tee adds, "If I hadn't made you stick to the rules."

• • •

Still, there is another side to my grandmother they never mention—a side familiar to me from the hours, days, and months spent in her company. Each weekday morning, till I was old enough to go to school, my mother dropped me off at Aunt Tee's on her way to work. When I arrived, Big Grandma was already puttering in the garden. I sat under a big mango tree while she brought me fresh fruit to go with my milk and toast. Sometimes there were fresh litchis or pomegranates. "This is what silkworms eat," she said, offering me a handful of purple mulberries. In mango season, when it was time to harvest the bright red and golden fruit, I helped to spot them among the shady branches and we picked mangoes until she had a fragrant apronful.

Sometimes in the afternoon, we went for a bus ride to the sweet shop and the dry goods store downtown. More often, though, we visited the sundry healers and prayer ladies in her acquaintance—including a clairvoyant herbalist and an acupuncturist nun—whose treatments eased the symptoms of her arthritis. She herself claimed the ability to heal with the energy flowing from her hands, and I can still see her, sitting up late into the night beside my sickbed, the touch of her cool palms upon my skin, while her lips move silently, chanting prayers.

When I ask my mother if she does not also have such memories, she says, "Even if Mama had been around, that's not the way it was for us."

"So, how was it?" I persist.

She explains that children were bound to their parents by duty and gratitude. Then she smiles. "Isn't it a pity that all that's changed?"

We have just come back from visiting Big Grandma and are sitting on the porch, drinking iced coffees. "You know, after Mama lost the use of her legs, it became too much for your aunt Tee," Mother begins.

"It would've been too much for anyone," I say.

"Back in the old days, though, we'd have kept her with us till the bitter end." She pauses to sip her coffee, and when she continues, there is an unaccustomed edge to her voice. "Of course, we are free of all that now."

I am remembering our visit to the home. The smell of disinfectant. The freezing air conditioning. The ancient residents in wheelchairs, lining the sunlit corridor. Today my grandmother thought she was on a ship, headed for somewhere she didn't know. "Where are we going?" she kept asking. "Why are you taking me there?"

My mother gazes out across the lawn and absently stirs the ice cubes in her glass. Finally, she turns to me. "When we are free," she asks, "what holds us then?"

• • •

While I am home, my mother cooks. On most mornings, when I come out into the kitchen, she greets me with the question, "What would you like for dinner tonight?" By the time I sit down to my first cup of coffee, she has already hung the laundry, swept and mopped the floors, and is taking a break, clipping recipes from the previous night's paper.

On other days, I wake to the smell of baking. A few mornings before Easter, a wonderful yeasty fragrance fills the whole house, and when I emerge from my bedroom, there are pans of sweet rolls cooling on every available surface in the living and dining rooms. Mother reminds me that they are having a bake sale for her General Electric cooking class, and while she was at it, she's decided to make extras to give away. None of it "penance food."

She believes that everything to do with eating should be a pleasure, and she takes as much care in selecting the food she will cook as in its actual preparation. When I am visiting, she rousts me out of bed on Wednesday mornings way before six, so we can get down to the open market when the produce vendors are setting up. Afterward, I drive her to Chinatown, where she is acquainted with the specialities of every shop. She sniffs and pokes, quizzes the vendors about prices, and periodically offers me bits of cryptic advice, like, "Buy fish whole," or "The sound of a pineapple tells you if it's sweet."

After my return to Michigan, Mother and I continue to keep in frequent touch. On one occasion, she reports that Big Grandma has now decided that she is visiting at her uncle's estate back in Japan. "She seems happier," Mother says. "But the last time I saw her, she complained of what a long stay it's been. Then she looked around at her roommate and the other residents out in the hall and whispered, 'What are all these people doing here?' "

During another call, my mother announces that she and Dad will be coming out to see us the following spring. It will be their first visit since we have moved to the Midwest.

She says, "I told your father that I'll be needing a whole new wardrobe for the trip."

"What you've got is probably fine," I say.

"It's not that." She hesitates. "Nothing fits."

My heart sinks a little. "What do you mean?"

She explains that she's been losing weight, then hastens to assure me, "I've been to the doctor and he's not concerned the slightest bit."

Every week she continues to lose another pound or two, but her monthly checkups turn up nothing unusual. She develops a bit of a backache, but both she and her doctor agree that it is just an old muscle strain flaring up.

In late March, when my father and she arrive for their scheduled visit, we are at the airport to meet them. At a distance, we can see them in the crowd, walking from the gate toward us. When I get a clear view, I am startled by the change in her. She is thin, very thin, and her clothes hang loosely on her small frame. Hal and I exchange looks and he squeezes my shoulder reassuringly. Then they spot us, too, and everyone is all smiles, exchanging hugs.

I take to watching her when she's not looking. Her color's good and, even with the weight loss, she does not *look* ill. But she seems to tire easily and her hands tremble, ever so slightly, when she unbuttons her jacket or picks up a pen to write. That night at dinner, the rest of us are passing the wine and helping ourselves to seconds when I notice that she hardly eats—just tiny bitefuls. "Come on, Mother, you've got to do better than that," I say.

She waves me off, but Dad joins in. "Can't keep your strength up if you don't eat."

Even Hal gets into the act and passes the chicken, which she ignores. She takes a tiny biteful of mashed potatoes from her plate.

Hal clears his throat. "So, how's the weather been in Honolulu?" Dad turns to answer him, but I continue watching Mother.

Finally she protests, "You've been staring at me all day. Now cut it out."

She is in such good spirits that it seems impossible anything can be wrong. She loves our little house. The crocuses blooming in the yard. The unpredictable spring weather. She loves that it can be seventy degrees and sunny one day, and snowing the next. When it starts to snow, she grabs her coat and boots so she can be outside in it. She crunches wet snow into little balls and throws them at us when my father and I step out the door. I take pictures of the two of them—in the snow on the front walk, in the snow on the side of the house, and in the snow in the backyard. Mother takes naps in the afternoon, but she is always up by dinner. She sits on a stool in the kitchen and watches while I cook. I teach her my recipes for tabouli and refried beans. When we go to the market, she piles the cart with asparagus, just coming into season, and that night we eat it cooked six different ways for our dinner.

She fills me in on the family news. Big Grandma is well, but lives almost entirely in her own world. Tee is baking more mango bread than ever. Esther has recently installed a five-thousand-dollar burglar alarm system, which, she claims, interferes with her telephone. "So whenever you call her, you get a busy signal," Mother explains. "And Esther says, 'If anyone has anything to say to me, they can just come here and tell me in person.'"

One afternoon, Hal drives us all to Lake Michigan. It is a forty-minute ride, and on the way over, my mother begins to sing. I remember summer evenings back in the Islands, when it was too hot to stay inside, and she and I went for drives along the sea. Then in the middle of telling me about some dance she'd been to when she was young, she'd start to sing, and I'd join in. We'd both sing, riding the night roads, all the way home.

A few weeks after my parents return to Honolulu, Mother takes to her bed. Her back is worse and she complains of "hunger pains" that don't go away even after she has eaten.

"Does she get out at all?" I ask my father.

"Only to the doctor," he says. "I'm doing all the housework now."

"Who does the cooking?"

There is a silence at the other end. "I do," he finally answers. "But I guess you could say she supervises."

I ask him to put her on the line, and she says, "You're always making such a fuss. There's nothing to be alarmed about."

"Have you thought of getting a second opinion?" I ask.

"A second, third, and fourth. . . ." She laughs. "No one's pushing the panic button."

In the weeks that follow, she continues going from doctor to doctor. They turn up nothing. They do X rays, barium swallows, and CAT scans. One performs an endoscopy and diagnoses gastritis. Another prescribes swimming therapy for her back condition. As long as no one mentions cancer, we are cheered by every diagnosis, but the weight continues slipping off.

I tell my father, "You have to feed her. We *have* to fatten her up."

And he replies, "She's lost her joy in food."

I begin making plans to fly out there when he calls to say that she has a fever and can't keep anything down.

She picks up the phone before he finishes talking. "Oh, Aya," she says. Her voice comes out in little gasps.

I try not to betray the panic I am feeling. "Just hold on; I'll be there soon. We'll get you better."

"I don't know what's wrong," she says.

These are the last words she speaks to me. That afternoon, my father drives her to the emergency room, and she is rushed into surgery. The doctor finds an abscess covering two-thirds of her liver. He inserts a drainage tube, then closes her up. "I've never seen anything like it," he says.

I fly back the next day. One of my cousins meets me at the airport, and we drive straight to the intensive care unit. My mother is in the same hospital where she had surgery two years before. When we arrive at the waiting room, my father and Aunt Tee are there. I put my arms around my father, who keeps saying, "We've been through this, I just know she's going to get better."

The rules of intensive care allow us to visit my mother in pairs for ten minutes, three times an hour, at twenty-minute intervals. She lies unconscious, with tubes running in and out of her body and a respirator to help her breathe. During one of the breaks between visits, I phone Hal in Michigan, and he says that he'll be with me soon.

Over the next few days, there is no change. Aunt Tee drops by again. The Birthday Girls come. The ladies from the General Electric cooking class bring food for our vigil. One afternoon I am alone with Mother when Aunt Esther enters the room. I look around for Aunt Tee, but Esther has come alone.

"I rode the bus," she says, positioning herself on the other side of the bed.

After we exchange a bit more small talk, I turn back to my mother and pick up where I left off. "Remember the time," I say to her, listing things we've seen and done.

A few minutes go by this way, when Aunt Esther suddenly speaks up; she has been remembering, too. She leans close to Mother's pillow and murmurs, "Remember when we were kids, and you got a new pair of shoes, and I didn't get any? Remember the lady at the corner store who gave you free ice cream that you never shared? Remember how you wanted to tag along wherever I went and how Mama beat me for not taking you?"

The next morning on my way to the ICU, I drop by the senior care wing to see my grandmother. The other residents are at their usual posts along the corridor, but she is parked in the lounge, in front of the TV set, which is playing a rerun of "Lassie."

"Hello, Grandma," I say, kneeling beside her.

She looks up from the image on the screen and peers at me. As I gaze back, it is as if I am looking at her through a one-way mirror. When she speaks, she uses the politest form of Japanese. "And who would you be?"

I begin to explain, then realize, with a kind of grief, that there is no explanation; she will never know anyone again.

I undo the string on the box of sweet bean cakes I have brought, then pass them to her, saying, "I remembered how you like these." Her face creases into a smile as she takes one out and bites into it. Then she offers one to me, and we sit for a while, eating quietly together. "This is a rare thing," she says, "Yes, this is a rare thing."

• • •

More days pass. Hal arrives. The doctors move Mother out of intensive care. It's not looking good, they say. The antibiotics aren't working, and the infection is in her blood.

In the new room, we can be with her all the time. We stand by the bed, massaging her icy hands and feet. Dad quits talking about miracle recoveries. One afternoon, while Hal is getting a cup of coffee and I am half-dozing in a chair across the room, I can hear my father talking to her. "It's okay, Betty," he is saying. "You can let go now. You can let go."

None of our friends or relatives comes by anymore. There is a sign on the door that says, VISITORS LIMITED TO IMMEDIATE FAMILY. I sense that it is difficult for my father to be there; the air conditioning, the hours of sitting on a hard chair are bad for his arthritis, so I tell him that it's all right if he leaves early because we'll call if anything happens.

When the nurses come to change the bedding, they instruct Hal and me to wear rubber gloves whenever we touch my mother. This is to safeguard against infection from the fluids leaking out of her. Periodically, someone stops by to vaccuum her mouth and throat with a suction device on the side of the bed. The necessity for doing this becomes more and more frequent, and finally, one of the nurses shows me how to do it. There is the smell of blood, perhaps of earth, around my mother's bed.

With just my husband there in the room with us, I sing to her. She lies in the same position she's been in, with her head turned to one side, and one leg slightly bent, as if she's dancing. I sing, "Sunset glow the day is over, let us all go home. . . ." I close my eyes, and imagine myself large—large enough to hold all of her, her dying, within me.

Hal and I have rented a room in the medical center where we can take quick naps during the day or grab a few hours of sleep at night. The room is in the same wing as the senior care facility, a floor below my grandmother's. At one or two in the morning, after a day of sitting with my mother, he and I squeeze into the narrow, twin-size bed, and still in our street clothes, almost immediately fall asleep. We have slept less than an hour when we are wakened by a banging on the door. We stumble to our feet, and I feel as if I've plunged into a pool of icy water. I am so cold, my teeth are chattering, and it is difficult to catch my breath. Hal steadies me, then opens the door. There are two nurses on the other side. They tell us, in a businesslike way, to go to my mother's room. As we follow them down the corridor, I think of Big Grandma somewhere upstairs, wakeful, among strangers.

The Weekend Travellers

It was midafternoon, hardly later than three, when Anna and Karl came to the house. They were following a sign they had seen by the roadside a mile or so back: POTTERY. They were not collectors, but the leafy Vermont roads, cool on this midsummer day, had so far been a pleasure to go along, winding, rising, gently falling, curving and rising again. However, the side road since the sign and the turnoff was little used. It was rutted, with weeds grown up so high they concealed the potholes and rattled beneath the fenders. Something crashed in the undergrowth to their right, running away. "Some animal," Karl said. But Anna thought it was somebody. She thought just now in terms of people, being hopeful of pregnancy, though he didn't quite know that.

A mile went by, then another. No further sign appeared.

Down from Canada on a long weekend holiday, married only a scant year, lovers (again) that very morning, they both experienced New England as pastoral, with a cool, uncrowded loveliness they remarked on, and were happy just to breathe its air. Maybe the place will be the charm, she thought, babies on her mind.

"Are you sure this was the right road?"

"I guess we'd better turn back."

Which one of them said these things scarcely mattered. They seemed the only thoughts to be had, and so the only things to say. The woods, as they stopped and wondered how to turn, had got thicker, stranger, wilder. Trees had grown to fantastic height with long bare trunks and fronded crests that took out large portions of the sky. Close by the road's tracks there was a thick encroachment of sumac and elderberry tangled with some other bushes Anna couldn't name. Looking down from the car window, she judged the growth as masking a declivity of uncertain depth. Now they were stuck for a place to turn. Karl put the car in gear and inched forward, hoping for a wider opening. Then at the road's next curve there it was, the house.

It was weatherworn, unpainted, with broad steps running up to the porch. A couple of wooden tables displayed pottery. No one was about.

• • •

Karl and Anna Wallens had met at a Montreal business colloquium where the prevailing language was French. Stumbling through a conversation at the social hour that followed, they discovered an absurd truth—they both were fluent in English. He was Polish, born there, but had stayed with relatives in Toronto to attend university. Anna Mendoza, born and reared in Spain, had an English mother, and had been sent off to school in the U.K. So it started between them. Later they dropped the *ky* off Wallensky. With marriage and rechristening, they had the feeling of rebirth. "In Canada," she observed to Karl, "one could be just anybody from anywhere—Iranian or Finnish or Czech." "What does it matter?" Karl would say. "We'll just be from nowhere." "Oh, but you must see Spain." "Maybe sometime," he would say. "Promise?" "Yes, promise." Anna often wore white, unsuitable for Montreal, but recalling to her the dry hills and flowering courtyards near Jerez. *I'll go back someday*, she vowed to herself. At work Karl was just Wallens. His slight accent merged with others.

For a little while they simply sat looking at what seemed an empty house. Finally they got out. Now the air was darker, shading toward twilight. From off in the woods behind the house, a little to the left by the sound of it, a dog was howling and barking urgently. Howl, then bark. Bark, then howl. It seemed ready to continue, for minutes or hours.

But here they were, and there on the porch was pottery. Karl and Anna mounted the steps. Knocking at the door, which stood open, brought no one. Within the depths of one large room, they could see more pottery displayed on a banquet-sized table, filling most of the space between windows and fireplace.

Someone came. A girl with an aging plain face, long sand-colored hair that looked never to have been either cut or combed, stained jeans and a man's shirt.

"Want something?"

"Oh, just to look. We saw your sign."

She did not reply but only waved a hand at the display and stood behind the table. Anna picked up a plate. The price, fifteen dollars, was scrawled on the bottom. Either Karl or Anna could have said it aloud: they were not comfortable here. There was something odd, though what, except for the unkempt road and the raucous dog, it would have pressed them to say. The girl stood looking at a broken fingernail with curiosity, as though it had nothing to do with her. The plate was a shallow gray crater, the size of a large dinner plate, balanced, smooth to the touch, in its plain way perfect.

"If you want it, get it," Karl said. He looked at the other objects with distaste. They were all marred by clumsy attempts to embellish them, some with animal motifs, Disney-like, and some with lettering of the His and Her sort. "Mary's Mug" with a funny face beneath. "Bill's Mug," etc. There were vases made of upended fish with open mouths, bookends of back-to-back squirrels, an endless succession of pitchers in every size, resembling frogs.

Anna decided to buy the plate and leave. Karl had no change for twenty dollars, nor did the girl. Karl and Anna made the sum up between them. "Do you have many customers?" Anna decided on conversation, a humanizing effort.

The girl did not glance up, but pulled at the ragged nail. "We take a lot of stuff into town."

"So you don't work all alone here?"

"Oh, no." Out back, the dog abruptly fell silent. The room seemed still as midnight.

"Well . . . thanks."

Karl and Anna began, as though by common consent, to back away, moving toward the door.

"I'll wrap it," the girl said, coming out of her distraction.

"It's okay." Anna felt suddenly that any delay in getting out of there was not to be considered.

As they reached the car, a noise from the road signaled the arrival of someone else, and before they could turn to leave, a pickup came jolting out of the woods and stopped just behind them. Two men, dressed in old jeans, got out. Only their beards distinguished them from one another, one being black and thick, the other a coppery thin scraggle needing a trim. They were going toward the house, scarcely glancing at Karl and Anna, who might have been invisible, not there at all.

"Excuse me, but you've blocked our way," Karl said. He spoke too loudly, in the tone of someone making an arrest.

Still, they did not look. One of them said, passing hurriedly up the steps, "Just in a minute." They went inside.

The Wallenses waited in the car. When insects drifted toward them through the dusky air, they rolled up the windows. From back of the house, the dog resumed barking. It was close in the car. Anna held the plate on her lap. It was rather heavy.

Karl finally got out and went up the steps to bang on the door. "You're blocking our way," he called. "Hallo! We can't get out." There was no answer. The place could have been deserted. It seemed to be getting later than it actually was. Karl came back down the steps. "The damnedest thing," he said.

"Let's try to drive past the truck," Anna suggested. "It can't be that impossible."

He walked around the pickup and looked into the bushes. Anna got out and joined him. The growth seemed too thick to deal with except with an ax maybe, a two-man saw, a machine for land clearing. She even checked the back of the pickup for any of those items and felt that if she had found one, she and Karl would have seized it and plunged into clearing the jungle. But nothing was visible except a pile of cloths, huddled together like old bedding, and several empty crates made of plywood.

"Shit." Karl said it with finality. He had started for the steps, when the red-bearded man emerged from around the corner of the house. He was grinning, reaching in his jeans pocket, evidently for the key. A dog was trailing at his heels. It was a police-type dog, small for the breed. It went snuffling, as though in an unfamiliar place.

"Sorry. I just forgot."

Karl stepped back, smiling now. Everything was okay. "We couldn't get out," he said, with a cordial note.

"I know, I know." Ramming his hand in one pocket after another, the man began to frown. "Hell, I guess he's got it."

"The key?"

"Yeah, the key." He turned around and moved off. "I'll be right back. Won't take a minute." He passed the corner of the house, the dog following. Again Karl and Anna sat and waited.

"Damn all this." Karl got out and slammed the door.

For some reason she said, "Don't."

"I've got to—" he began but did not finish. As he strode angrily up the steps and into the house, she noticed the patches of sweat in his black hair. Anna heard him calling. "Hey! We need the key! Hey!" She pushed up the blond gathering of hair from her neck. It was damp from the heat.

There was never such a surrounding silence. In it, she heard his footsteps stamp through the house to the back, then a slamming door. Descending steps, then silence again. She sat in the car and wondered, *Why am I so frightened?*

By the time she at last got from the car and walked toward the steps, she had the curious feeling of not knowing her own size. She could have been walking on stilts, nine feet tall; she could have been the squashed-down height of a midget. She mounted the steps as he had done, passed through the door, the large silent room with the animal pots. She pushed through the back door. It gave onto a porch, high from the ground, identical with the front, so that except for the display tables, the house could have been swung back to front on a swivel and no difference would have appeared.

The backyard stretched out before her, sloping sharply down to a sagging fence with a gate, standing open. No one was in sight. The sun was moving below the treetops. Anna called Karl, but her voice was taken up by the expanse of yard, and struck the line of trees and growth just beyond the fence too faintly even to echo. She tried again, but the echo was meager.

Why not go on, through the gate, follow the path into the woods? No, the thing to do was find a telephone inside, call that number (911), the police (she didn't know how), the operator (that should be easy). He had been gone too long, but how long? The day was lowering fast, yet her watch showed an early hour. It might have stopped, but did she know? On the phone, she would invent something, exaggerate.

Just then, from the long fall of the woods to the right, she heard voices. The words were indistinguishable. Their rise and fall had the rhythm of a discussion; their quality seemed male with only the occasional higher note of what might have been a woman. Anna called again. "Karl!"

She would run down the steps, she would run toward the voices. They stopped suddenly.

She was standing on the steps. From somewhere in the woods toward the left, the dog began to bark again, then howl. Howl, then bark. Was it the same dog they had seen? Why hadn't it gone where the people were?

Will I scream? she wondered.

Halfway down the steps, Anna sat. To her surprise, she saw that she had brought along the plate. It rested heavily on her lap. She rubbed her fingers on the smooth gray surface. It felt cool.

From nearby in the woods a number of birds, gathered together, were twittering in a rhythm much like conversation. The sound was soothing because it was so companionable, like questions and answers around a favored child who might be sleeping. The voices began again and so did the dog, but both had receded to a farther distance. Yet the birds seemed nearer.

Anna sat quietly on the steps, listening. A small eternity caught and held, as strong as life or death.

"The key fell among the leaves," said the birds. "They are searching for it. The dog is barking at a squirrel. Soon he will go to them. They will all come back to you. Wait and see."

A Christmas Card

S now began falling sometime shortly after midnight, although Alan didn't notice it then, and wouldn't have noticed it now except that a draft shook the slats of the venetian blind just enough to disturb him. He looked up from a letter he was trying to start. A fringe of mist condensed around the window, and the view from his sofa had a soft, bleary focus. He rose, crossed the room, and raised the blind, pressing his face against the glass. Outside, snow slanted past his window, falling in darkness until it was briefly illumined under the cone of blue light from the street lamp. The streets were white and flashing with cold chips of crystal. He hadn't realized snow was predicted. He hadn't realized how late it was, either.

For most of the night, he'd busied himself with listening to an album of baroque Christmas music and working on a letter. In a dreamy and pensive mood, nearly baroque itself, he played the simple variations of Johann Pachelbel's *Canon* over and over again. The record had belonged to Josalyn. Wadded balls of pale-blue stationery lay on the bare wood floor around the sofa. The letter, to his mother, was not going well. Yesterday had been the Feast of the Epiphany, and it touched off a twinge of nostalgia. He liked to fancy himself a writer, and occasionally he struggled with a script, or wrote an article, but right now he was having a hard time scribbling this simple letter, and in the middle of so many false fitful starts, he'd craved a baked potato, and two of them were roasting in the oven. "Roasting" was how he thought of the potatoes. Now made aware of the falling snow, the potatoes sounded tastier that way.

Alan lowered the blind. His apartment was small. On the white walls there were art prints, most of them leftover from college, all of them nicely framed, although they hung off kilter, at odd, tortured angles. That was because the apartment itself was composed entirely of skew lines. There wasn't a plumb wall in the place. When Alan first moved in, he noticed he was always leaning one way or the other, vaguely searching out true vertical. He never found it. Earlier in the night, he'd thought of moving to a better place, but he couldn't imagine where he'd go.

His mother had called the day before to say that she was thinking about him. She wanted to let him know, too, that the Magi had arrived safely in

Bethlehem. The journey of the Magi was a drama they played out every year, a routine from his childhood. Alan and his brothers and sisters could watch the Magi wandering through the house and know that Christmas was coming soon. They began their journey on the sill above the kitchen sink, and the holiday season was officially finished on the Feast of the Epiphany when, at last, they made it to the manger, above the fireplace; his mother would arrange a nice supper, and they'd fete the Wise Men, and after that, the vacation was over, and it was time to get on with the business of life. Immediately, his mother would take all the decorations down and throw out the tree. She still did this, even though no one lived at home anymore. He had the image of his mother stealing through the dark, quiet house alone, pushing the Wise Men forward, inch by inch, and day by day.

Alan looked at the letter, a quarter page of black scrawl that fell to a blank space of blue in midsentence. What was there to say? Christmas morning he opened the package his mother had mailed him weeks before, thinking it was funny how he'd waited. Because she had sent a present, he'd gone out and bought a small tree to put it under. After he set up the tree, he cut snowflakes and pasted loops of green and red construction paper together in a long chain and fashioned a tiny angel out of a rolled cone of purple paper with gold wings stapled to it and a misshapen foil head wedged into the small opening at the tip. The angel he made was a seraphim, with six wings. He taped chocolate kisses to the tree for ornaments. In the package from his mother was a gold-plated pen and the pale-blue stationery and a card saying Merry Christmas and please write a brief note letting me know how you are. But Alan didn't know what to say.

When the timer rang, he opened the oven door and jabbed his potatoes with a fork. They burned him when he pulled them off with his bare hand, and steam rose in frail curls through the small holes the tines made. He looked through the cabinets, but the last of the foil had gone to make his seraphim. He pulled the angel's head off, and carefully unfolded the balled-up sheet of foil and wrapped his potatoes. He put on his coat and scarf and black watch cap. He couldn't find his gloves, but it didn't matter. He placed a hot potato in each pocket. At the last minute, on his way out, he grabbed the salt and pepper shakers from his small dining table, shut off the lights, and went down the stairs and into the street for a walk.

The city was empty, as if uninhabited, and yet, as Alan walked, looking into the massed, swirling sky, every distance was filled with falling snow, and the frantic descent, the crowded way the white flakes flurried as they emerged from the dark sky into the light of the streetlamps, made for a fullness that was at odds with the early hour and the cold and the silence. Alan hunched his shoulders against the wind, holding a baked potato in the palm of each hand. They were quite hot. He couldn't hold them for long. He let them rest in his pockets until his hands got cold, and then he held them again.

He walked toward the park. The houses were still dark and quiet and seemed empty, although here and there, a light glowed through a window and someone's shadow would pass. Snow cut across the warm light like another kind of shadow. The flakes were larger now, and in the driving wind they traced an endless, shifting pattern of ornate scrolls through the air. Garbage cans lined the streets, and every few houses a Christmas tree lay tipped over or propped up against an iron gate, often with stray glistering strands of tinsel still hanging from them. The deepening snow on the sidewalk drifted smoothly against the garbage cans and boxes of rubbish and flocked the dry yellowing branches of the trees. Apparently, other people waited until the Epiphany to throw out their trees, too.

He kicked the untracked snow with his boots, watching the small explosions of powder as he walked on. Under the streetlamps, the snow was like diamonds, but in the park, the lamps were different, and the snow glittered like a sea of gold. The lamps in the park were ornamental reproductions of gaslights, which burned with a fake yellow flame. The flight of the snow had a golden filigree to it, making a tracery that repeated itself so swiftly and insistently, so perfectly, that it hung suspended and still in the light, as if draped in place.

In the center of the park was a concave band shell. A big star made of white Christmas lights shone brightly above the roof. Garlands of fir wreathed the gutters, and red plastic bells swayed soundlessly under the eaves.

Alan didn't see the man until he'd passed him and begun walking toward Main Street. The man leaned over the railing, under cover of the band shell.

"Excuse me? Sir?"

Alan, lost in thought, jerked around. The man came toward him.

"Yes?" said Alan.

"You wouldn't have a light, would you?" the man asked. He was small and fat with thick ears and rheumy pink eyes that were nearly shut. The hem of his overcoat swept the ground, and a frozen rim of ice clung to it. Snow landed on his hatless head and stuck to his hair.

"No, I'm sorry, I don't," said Alan.

The man shivered and stuffed his hands into his pockets.

"It's sure cold," he said. He looked around. "I don't see what you're doing out here."

"Just walking," Alan said. "I couldn't sleep."

"I was sleeping," said the man, "but now I'm not."

"I wish I had a light for you," Alan said.

There wasn't anything else to say. Through a thick tangle of trees, beyond the park and across the street, there was a church with sharp spires and a high, square bell tower, and a white statue of the Virgin.

"Is it supposed to snow all night?" Alan asked.

"I don't know."

"Looks like it. Looks like it'll fall all night."

Alan sniffed and the air tasted good.

"Where do you stay?" he asked.

"Here. The mission. Different places."

"Why don't you go to the mission now?"

"I don't like it there all the time," he said. "You pray for everything. You pray for oatmeal."

Alan shrugged.

"I get tired of it."

"Are you hungry?" Alan asked.

"I don't know," he said. "I hadn't thought about it."

"Well?"

"I guess so. I guess I am, if I think about it."

"Would you like a baked potato?"

"Ah, sure."

"You don't sound sure."

"Why not? Hell, why not?"

"I've got one right here," said Alan.

Alan pulled one of the baked potatoes out of his pocket. He held the shining silver ball of foil like a precious gift he'd produced, magically, out of nowhere, for the little man to behold. The man stared at the bright wrapping, which sparkled under the star's light. Snowflakes fell and dissolved on the hot tinfoil.

"You're shittin' me," he said. "Are you shittin' me?"

"Would I lie about something like this?" Alan asked.

The man thought about this for a moment. "No, probably not."

"Besides the proof is right here, isn't it? Tell me this isn't a baked potato."

Alan unwrapped the baked potato, and steam swirled up through the falling snow.

"Here's your potato."

"Thanks."

"Wait. Don't eat yet."

Alan reached into his pocket. "Salt and pepper?" he asked.

"Sure."

"Say when." Alan salted the potato lightly, and then doused it in black pepper.

"Spices and everything. You come prepared."

"The salt's for wisdom," said Alan, "and the pepper's so you aren't bored to death. Potatoes can be boring."

Alan watched him as he bit into the potato. "It's hot. Jesus. Good though, very good. Nice and warm." His eyes watered up. "You're some kind of guy."

Alan decided to eat his potato later. He touched the man's shoulder.

"Enjoy," he said.

"I will," the guy said, swallowing the hot potato, "I am!"

Alan walked away and was about at the park's edge when the man yelled. "Hey, my name's John," he screamed.

"I'm Alan," Alan screamed back.

He stopped at a doughnut shop and drank a quick cup of sweet hot chocolate, left a decent tip, and started home. The snow fell even harder now, and it lay thickly over the sidewalks and streets, and covered up the usual litter, and everything was soft and white, with a kind of calm, equable look to it, a stillness and poise, as if all the old lines and divisions had been erased, and a person could start fresh, begin anew. Christmas decorations were still up along Main Street. Big candy canes hung from the streetlamps, gaily festooned with green and red streamers, and plastic snowmen in black top hats clung to the poles with one hand, and waved straw brooms high in the air with the other. On every corner, tinny gray speakers crackled and hummed in the cold air, blurting out Christmas carols, like a choir of dime-store angels. As Alan crossed an empty intersection, the speaker was playing "Joy to the World." The words drifted in the air and sank like the giddy swoon of angels in flight.

Already, though it was still dark, people had begun to stir, and more lights were lit up in the houses along Main Street. Perhaps because of the weather, people were leaving early for work, or perhaps they were always up at this hour. Alan didn't know. He bought a cup of coffee at the all-night deli, thinking maybe John could use some by now. As he was leaving, the Indian man behind the register asked Alan if he would mind doing him a small favor.

"My dear brother is returning to India today," he said, "and we would, please, like to take a photograph. Of me, and my two brothers. We want Mother to see the store. We want her to see how things are with us in America."

"Sure," said Alan, "no problem."

The man waved to his two brothers, and all three came around from behind the counter. The first Indian man had a Polaroid camera. He handed it to Alan.

"Outside," he said.

All of them, including Alan, stepped outside into the snow. The three brothers stood together on the sidewalk in front of the store. They linked their arms together and flashed broad white grins. Alan futzed with the camera, fumbling for the button. When he looked through the lens, the three brothers shrank and seemed very far away. He found the button and clicked. The bulb exploded in a burst of blue, and a grinding gear spat out a picture. All of them huddled together, bending their heads to watch it develop, but before it could, through the small opening in their huddle, a snowflake lit precisely where the head of the departing brother would have been. Everything developed, quite slowly in the cold, except this brother's head. There was an eerie white space, an emptiness, where the snowflake fell.

Also, Alan apparently jiggled the camera, and the shot was poorly framed. All the brothers leaned at a funny, seasick angle. They all looked at the photo. They all groaned.

"Let's do it again," said Alan. "That was just practice."

"Yes," said the first Indian, "once more."

"Inside," said the brother whose head had been blotted out. "It's too cold."

Alan imagined that he was sore about the accident to his head, which, however random and innocent, must have seemed portentous, like a jinx, on the eve of a long journey. Alan wanted to put him at ease and devised a brief homily.

"Every snowflake," said Alan, "is unique, even the very smallest ones. Absolutely individual, like a human being, a soul. Even though they all look the same when they're falling down, under closer inspection, under a microscope, you discover this is just not true. You should consider this accident a good sign, a prophecy, a singular blessing on your trip."

"Perhaps," said the brother who was leaving. "But I'm freezing my balls off. Let's go inside, please."

"No," said the brother who hadn't spoken yet.

The three brothers bunched together again and flashed broad grins, and Alan fumbled with the camera and managed to hold it level, and finally the bulb burst the darkness with a lovely blue explosion, and the gear moaned and gave forth a photograph once more. Alan covered it quickly. When they dared to look, the picture was vague and still developing, but all the heads seemed to be there, neatly perpendicular, and the picture was going to look right, and everyone was more than happy.

Even though he went home along the same route, the falling snow had obliterated his tracks, and it was as if he were going a different and entirely new way, as if he had never been there before. When he got to the park, John was gone. Alan hoped he was warm and sleeping safely. He drank John's coffee under the star that sat perched above the silent band shell. The scene before him was immaculate and beautiful; he wanted to feel that unalloyed purity, like the snow was innocent of itself as it fell. The park was quiet, but when Alan stood inside the band shell, he could hear the distant sound of the ocean, of sea surf crashing far away, as if he'd cupped a small shell over his ears. Where the wading pool used to be, two dolphins swam in the sea of gold snow. In the summer, children rode the dolphins, and the dolphins spouted water into the pool. Now, in the snow, they looked like walruses. As he stood there, more and more lights flicked on in the houses surrounding the park. A grayish dawn began to dissolve the dark night, and the sea of gold dimmed and faded. When the star flicked off, Alan walked on.

He still held true to his plan, trying to retrace his steps, and still there was no trace of them. In the vague distance he thought he heard something like a foghorn keening at regular intervals, but he wasn't sure. For the second time that night he passed Josalyn's building. He stood on the sidewalk and stared up at the door. Then he climbed the steps and rang her bell. He waited.

"Hello?" he heard through the speaker.

"It's me," he said. "Can I come up?"

There was a silence, and then, deep within the speaker, he could hear the hollow sound of someone asking, "Who is it, Joss?"

There was another silence. Then Josalyn said, "I'm not alone."

"Oh," Alan said. It was precisely what he had suspected, and yet he was absolutely surprised. He was stunned.

"What time is it?" Josalyn asked. "Is something wrong?"

"No," Alan said.

"What do you want?"

Coming toward him, he heard the loud, rough grinding of a garbage truck and saw men with big barrels running back and forth in front of the headlights. The headlights cut an intense beam through the murky light. All down the street, as they came closer, Alan saw them hauling Christmas trees to the truck.

He could hear Josalyn's scratchy voice through the speaker, calling: "Are you there? Hey, are you there?"

Alan listened to the warning blast of the foghorn and watched the garbagemen. They dumped their loads into the truck, flipped a switch, and a motor groaned and the garbage was crushed, and the headlights dimmed under the strain until it was done, and then brightened again. A man in a yellow rubber suit snatched up a nearby tree. Needles shook from it as he pitched the dry, dead tree into the truck. Alan watched it crumple and disappear. He was starting to feel cold. The truck and the running men went down the street, farther and farther away, hauling off Christmas trees.

When he got home, Alan remembered his baked potato. He pulled it out of his pocket. He also had the Polaroid of the headless Indian. He'd keep it as a souvenir. The picture actually looked like a tableau vivant or one of those antique photo amusements, where a person steps behind a cardboard scene, and pokes his head through a hole, and gets a souvenir snapshot of himself doing something novel and extraordinary. If he could find a small enough picture of himself, he'd cut it out and paste his own head in there. He hoped the Indian would have a safe journey. He tacked the Polaroid to the wall. It was hard — no, it was impossible to line up. He stepped back and looked at it. He shifted it slightly, and stepped back farther, and looked again. If he stared at the square white border that framed the snapshot, the picture was cockeyed, but if he concentrated on the leaning brothers, they seemed as upright and plumb as could be. He left it alone. In a room like that, it didn't pay to dwell too long on any one thing.

He relit the pilot light on his heater and turned the gas up high. The blue flames from the heater always mesmerized Alan exactly as if they were a real fire in a fireplace. He put on Pachelbel again and stretched himself out on the sofa. It had a bed underneath it, but these days he rarely went to the trouble. His potato was cold on the outside, but when he cracked it open, it was still hot and steaming in the center. He gave it a light salting and peppered it generously. He was famished. The potato burned his lips, and he slowed down, and when he slowed down, it was good. It was the best, most memorable baked potato he'd ever had. He heaped more black pepper on the last few bites and ate them, then stared at the blue flames, then out the window at the falling snow.

He got up and turned over the Pachelbel on the turntable. He pulled out the bed beneath his sofa. Laid with old sheets, it was already made. He slipped off his shoes and his shirt and pulled off his pants and socks and quietly set them beside the heater. He turned the gas up a notch so it would be nice and warm when he woke, and then he drew back the top sheet, easing it away gently. He turned the lights off and could again see the falling snow sink slowly past the window, circling down.

But when the record ended, it was too quiet, and he played Pachelbel one last time. The variations were actually quite monotonous in that fancy, baroque manner, but he sort of liked the monotony, the gentle sameness, the way the *Canon*'s variations repeated themselves, wandering, building up, yet always leading him back, in the end, to some already familiar place. He turned the volume down low. He put the stationery away and set the cap back on his gold-plated pen. There really wasn't anything to say, at least nothing that couldn't wait until tomorrow, or the day after. Tomorrow, or the day after, he'd remember to tell his mother how everyone in the world, it seemed, tossed out their trees on the Feast of the Epiphany.

He was a day late. He pulled his seraphim off the small tree and set it aside on the kitchen table. He took the tree over to the window. He raised the blind and opened the window and looked out. The garbagemen hadn't made it to Alan's street yet. Dozens of Christmas trees, propped upright or fallen over, lined the sidewalks. Leaning out the window, Alan thought he heard the foghorn, and he knew he heard something, and it sounded like a cry of warning, of some urgency, but it wasn't a foghorn, he didn't think, because he wasn't anywhere near water. In fact, he was far inland. He looked up and down the street, plucked a last kiss from the tiny tree, and let it fall.

Burning Luv

The cowboy hadn't even said good-bye; he took off while I was under the bridge taking a leak. He got out just long enough to toss my backpack onto the shoulder and then he was gone, just like that. I walked back and picked it up, a little light-headed from the beer and reefer we'd been putting away, and wondered why he had dumped me. We had been talking nonstop, and the silence that fell after his little white truck crested the far hilltop seemed too hollow for an outdoors type of quiet. It felt like the quiet you might hear inside a bathroom late at night in a bus station. It was a quiet that hurt, the way dying alone in the snow might hurt. Except that here it was hot and I was high and my pack seemed heavier than it had been before. It all the sudden seemed a dead weight, and I was tempted to just dump it, the way the cowboy had dumped me, in the desert by the side of the road. I didn't, though, after all; I hefted it and tried to figure my situation.

There was some traffic coming from the east but nothing in my direction. The interstate was new and black, as if it had just spilled from the back of the truck and hadn't had time to bleach out and dust over. I-70 through Utah and west Colorado was like that—most of the truckers avoided it, went north on 80 if they were heading to San Francisco or south on 40 to L.A. Nobody much used this stretch, and I was wondering if I'd be sleeping outside that night. There were some mesas off the roadway that looked close enough to walk to; a fire on the far side wouldn't attract attention. But I didn't like the desert, and I knew I didn't want to wake up still in it.

Lately I'd been having dreams about walking through the desert. There were dead fish and busted-spine wooden boats everywhere, one or two of the fish still flipping around. Snails as big as cats slipped along, looking for shade, and the ground was covered with clumps of soggy, flat-leaved amber weeds, drying to a high stink. Somewhere I had heard that the desert used to be all underwater, a gigantic sea bigger than all the oceans put together, cruised by dinosaur fish and eels the size of tankers. But out in the real desert there were no puddles, no mud, nothing but dirt and small, flat stones. The air dried out the inside of your nose, cracked your lips, and made your spit taste alkaline. Here and there was a lizard or a roly-poly bug, but they weren't much for company. Any birds you saw flew in high arcs, horizon to horizon; they might have been jets.

Along about an hour came a Jeep. He pulled it over and I liked the fact he had a gas tank strapped to the back, so right off I showed him my nine millimeter and marched him out about a mile into the desert, bouncing along behind him in the Jeep. I was feeling easy still from the pot, so I didn't let him think he had anything to worry about, bullet-wise. I even let him keep his thermos, although it only had coffee in it, and found him a Mars bar from a paper bag on the floor. I told him how it all worked, how if he prayed for me he could probably find his wheels in Grand Junction or even Denver if I felt adventurous. He prayed—they always pray when they think they're getting their machine back as part of the deal—and I left him there on his knees with a piece of advice about rattlesnakes and hitchhikers: Don't pick either of them up.

The Jeep was one of those older ones that tended to flip, so right away I strapped myself in under the roll bar and flipped it, just for fun. The Jeep stopped up on its side, and I had to unstrap myself and drop to the ground, then shove the thing over. Right off the bat I was sorry. The gas tank had been flung off the back and ruptured: a bad omen. I kicked the side of the Jeep and cursed myself. It was a good idea to avoid getting gas in other people's cars, especially if they're hard-borrowed. Gas in a can was a blessing, and I had ruined it. Those Jeeps get maybe fifteen on a good day.

I got back out on the interstate about the time I started to come down. My stomach was rising up on me, empty and hot, and my head hurt with the wind whipping around my ears. The sun was dead behind me, nearly down, setting off the scenery with bands of orange. The sky was the burnt-blue color of a rifle barrel. I began to hate the cowboy hard for what he did to me and brought the Jeep up to eighty. He had a good lead, but his little Jap pickup wasn't good for more than fifty-five.

We'd gotten together in the basement of a VFW outside of Salt Lake—a Brigham Young football game was on the TV, and we were both bad-mouthing the home team from different ends of the bar. In the whole place there was only a short, neckerchiefed barmaid, and between us at the bar a couple of old purplenoses with windbreakers and watery eyes talked with hunched backs about their problems with the VA.

"Now how about *that* fat-ass," the cowboy was saying, pointing up at the TV. "Goddamn Mormons ought to just stay out of sports altogether, if you ask me."

The barmaid glowered at him. "Hey, there, language," she said. She looked at me like I was the type to agree with her.

He ignored her and yelled at the TV. "Hey, that's a ball, not a Bible, you great big stupid shit." He was a tall, thin guy with a strange, happy face and a mustache that trailed down to the corners of his chin. He had a ponytail. He was smoking cigarettes that he bought one at a time from the barmaid, blowing the smoke into the top of his glass before he drank.

They showed a cheerleader right then, and he took off his cowboy hat and slammed it against the stool next to him. "Hooee," he said, "like to bite her on the ass, get lockjaw, and have her drag me to death."

"Hey," said the barmaid. "Language, I said."

I pounded my fist on the bar. "No shit, buddy. Watch your fuckin' mouth."

She pointed a thick finger to the wall. "I got a phone, you know."

Then she walked over to me, smiling hard and unfriendly.

"Son," she said, "we don't want no trouble. Can you maybe get your friend to settle down some?"

I looked over at the two purplenoses and they looked into their beer glasses quick. "Which one, Mom?" I asked.

Her lips pulled back over her teeth. "I got a phone," she said again. And just like that a couple of highway troopers wandered down the stairs, and the barmaid's face went all smug and hateful.

"*Boyyyys*," she said.

The cowboy and I sort of stretched and pulled ourselves off the barstools. On the way up the stairs he reached into a slit in the collar of his coat and pulled out a middle-sized black switchblade. It was a nice, slick move; I hadn't noticed the bulge under his ponytail. Outside, while I fished my pack from the bushes where I'd hid it, he stuck the knife in the tire of the patrol car, easy as you please, and it spit out steam quick like a cough. We hopped in his little Jap pickup and left with the lights out, heading southeast toward mine country, laughing and carrying on about bars and cops and Mormons in general. On the whole it was a fine time, finer than I'd had since I could remember.

After a few miles of this and that, I noticed on the seat next to me a leather satchel, the throat open, and the inside was full of round, flat tins of makeup and a bright-red wig. I pulled out the wig and held it up around my fist.

"What kind of cowboy wears a wig?"

"The clown kind," he said. "When I can't get a ride, I clown." I looked at him blank and he took the wig from my hand. "Rodeo," he said, stuffing it back in the satchel. "And in the winter maybe your occasional liquor store."

We slept that night in the back of the truck, between horse blankets, with his coat for a pillow. He'd had to hoist his saddle up onto the roof to make room, and after things settled down I noticed one of the stirrups was hanging down over the rear window like a noose, and if I moved my head just right, I could get the full moon to shine right through the center of it, all the way through the cab. After a while it was gone, up and west, and it wasn't long before the cowboy snored me to sleep, his hand on the small of my back. I slept good; it was the first night in a long time that I didn't have the desert dream.

Back when I was married, after the navy horseshit, I thought that making money was the thing to do. I never cared much for Lia, one way or another, but she was Filipino and didn't expect much and didn't ask questions. Her family had given me a thousand dollars to marry her and take her to the States. After I got out of Leavenworth, I brought her over. Everything went okay for a while until one night she came at me with a kitchen knife, screaming over and over she was going to "cutoff you dickey, cut off you dickey." I lit out of there and never looked back.

If not for the dishonorable I'd have gone back to the navy. Truth is, they barely took me the first time, and I'd gone in begging, let me tell you. None of that jungle infantry shit for me. The ship they stuck me on was nothing more than a gray coconut, bobbing in the South China Sea for three months at a time—it hated me and I hated it back. I was lucky, though; I had a mate named Cecil and we got along fine. He was a rancher's kid from North Dakota, just as gentle as can be, but then he went and stabbed me in the arm when I told him about me and Lia getting married back in Manila. That night he loaded himself with foul-weather gear and metal doodads hooked to his belt, and under a full moon he hopped off the coconut, his hands above his head. The duty watch saw him; he said the boy slid under the waves like a butter knife into dirty dishwater. None of my mates said anything, but I got the ticket anyway; I couldn't explain the wounds on my arm. Contributing to the death of a sailor, they called it, not being able to prove the other thing. I was in Kansas in less than a month.

Later, when I was living with Lia in the trailer, I started writing those letters to Cecil. Since he was dead and I didn't want them lying around, I got the smart idea of sending them to Santa Claus, care of the north pole. I'd heard that somebody actually read those letters, somebody at the post office or somewhere, looking for kids who say they're being beat by their folks. So I just wrote to Cecil, asking him about how things were down there, under-neath all the waves. I told him about how the whole thing with Lia was just for the money, and I retold it every time, in every letter. It was one of those letters that Lia found, when she, too, came at me with a knife. Man, it's some-thing, being stabbed. Not many people can say they been stabbed. The worst part is the itching when it starts to heal. It invites you to tear it open, get it all infected inside. The body doesn't forgive you letting something into it like that; it knows it'll never heal right again.

After we crawled out of the back of the truck that next morning, we drove into Price and ate eggs and ketchup and coffee in a place by the side of the road. The cowboy told me about his wife, that she was part Indian, and she had been raped by her half brothers more times than she could remember. He showed me a picture of her someone had made into a postcard. It was in black and white, grainy like it was a hundred years old. The girl in the picture looked about thirteen. The back of the postcard said: *Girl in Traditional Ceremonial Dress, 1970*.

The cowboy took his wig in his hand and shook it, brushing it the way he might brush a horse. "I'm supposed to send her money every month," he said. "But I don't. I'd be in prison stealing the money I'm supposed to send her. Last time I saw her she said those brothers of hers were out looking for me. They're tribal police and they're allowed to kill me on sight if they want."

The cowboy got quiet then, and after a minute it looked like he was having trouble swallowing. Halfway through his eggs he turned and ran into the bathroom. When he came out he was sweaty and one of his eyes was deep red, like he'd poked it hard. I pointed to it and asked him what was wrong with it.

"Nothing's wrong with it," he said, looking peeved. "It's the other one."

The other was white, blue in the middle. "It looks fine," I said.

"It better. It cost six hundred dollars."

I stared at it again, and I was sorry that it was so much nicer than the real one. He shook his head and poked around at his hard eggs. Then he looked up at me.

"Goddamn, I'm scared to death of those Indians," he said. "It's so I can't even show up at a rodeo anymore, afraid they'll be there waiting. I don't even know what they look like. Every Indian I see has me reaching for my knife."

I didn't say anything. I was from Illinois, and the thought of a cowboy this afraid of Indians impressed the hell out of me. I thought about that slit in his collar and I was glad he had it there. If anybody needed to get to a knife quick, he did.

"I'm going to Texas," he said. "They got rodeo and I understand there's no Indians down there no more."

"Hell," I said. "I never seen a rodeo before. I'll go with you."

He didn't say anything. He picked up his cowboy hat and put it on his head. I paid for the breakfast and got into the truck. We headed down south, meaning to catch the interstate by midday. We ate a few pills he had lying around in the truck, drank a few beers, partook of some weed. My head started buzzing, and it got eerie when we dropped down and were in the desert officially. The valley we came into was hollow and flat, with carrier-shaped buttes on either side. Then suddenly down ahead of us lay the black ribbon of the interstate with a few bright sparkles moving across the length of it. The highway we were on was rough and bumpy, and we bobbed around quite a bit in the little truck, but with the interstate in sight it looked like smooth sailing just ahead, all the way to Texas.

I was so grateful for the cowboy's company and grateful for the truck and the interstate and glad that I wouldn't be left in the desert alone to fend for myself. Things had been bad but they were looking up, looking up for the both of us. I would help him with his Indian problems and he would see me through the desert. Things were going to be fine, I was sure of it. Only, I hadn't noticed right off that the cowboy hadn't been saying much. I didn't notice because I'd been talking nonstop ever since breakfast, even about Cecil, of all things.

I should have paid more attention; it was five minutes later that the cowboy dumped me by the side of the road.

It was about thirty miles outside of Grand Junction that I saw the little white truck, pulled over to the side of the interstate, smoke billowing up from under the hood. It was nearly dark and I turned off the lights of the Jeep. I could just see the cowboy off a ways into the desert, against the wire fence, looking southeast toward Texas. He was a dark patch against the smooth white cover of the desert. I pulled up quiet behind the burning truck. I took the nine millimeter from under the seat and when I got out, stuffed it in the back waistband of my jeans. He hadn't even turned around.

I walked up to about ten feet behind him and cleared my throat. He turned slowly, and his face went confused when he saw me. He looked behind me at the Jeep. It was a few seconds before he looked me in the eye again. He was already scared and that suited me. I had liked him a lot but now I couldn't remember why.

"Hey, partner," he said. His voice was squeaky. "You come around just in time."

"Looks like it." I said.

He nodded over at the smoldering truck without taking his good eye off me. "Isn't that a bitch? Threw a rod."

"They'll do that."

"Yeah," he said, "they sure will. Where'd you get that Jeep?" He asked it in that way that didn't expect an answer. I just stared at him and didn't say anything. The light was nearly all gone and the gun was getting cold against my back. As he started to say something else I reached back and pulled it out. I figured it was the right time. He stopped in his tracks.

"Hey," he said "What's this for?"

"What's this for? You just took off, threw my bag onto the dirt and took off."

"You were talking crazy." His good eye darted around a little as he spoke, like it might have been following a fly. "Some wild faggot navy shit about a drowned guy." As soon as he said this he licked his lips and his eyes slowed down. He reached behind and scratched the back of his neck. When he spoke again his voice was smoother. "You got to understand, I'm a wanted man. It wasn't anything personal."

I pointed the nine at his forehead. "Sounds personal as all get out to me."

It had a good effect. His eyes flew wide open and his mouth dropped. He shook his head, and his eyes both stared at the pistol.

"You're with them Indians?" he said. His voice was high and terrified. "You are, aren't you?"

It was so crazy I wanted to laugh, but for some reason I couldn't. Instead, I felt my throat start to tighten, and my eyes got blurry. The air had grown cold; I shivered. I waved the pistol and made my voice hard.

"Kneel on the ground over here, back to me."

He came over slow and knelt in the dust in front of me, his back bowed, the knuckles of his spine pressed out under his T-shirt. He started to cry; his ribs pulsed out from his sides like gills, and he began to sway a little. I stepped up behind him, took off his hat, and put the nose of the gun gently against the back of his head, where his hair pulled together into the ponytail. Some white light flowed over him—a truck on the road behind us—and my shadow slid across his back. I pressed the gun against the soft underside of the ridge of his skull, and his shoulders stiffened, his back arched, and he let out a small moan that made my head swirl.

"You should have never left like that," I said. "Why'd you do that?"

"God," he said, "tell her I'll come back, I promise."

"Hush, now." The hate was flowing from me. "It's too late for her now." The sun had dropped and the air around us was now black, thick, and cold. My hands were numb and my legs ached.

"Here's what you do," I told him. "Just pretend you're swimming in the ocean." My voice was nearly a whisper. "You're swimming in the ocean, but you're getting weak." I heard him sob, and I knew then that I wanted him to sink, that he *had* to sink. I lifted up the ponytail to do him at the top of the neck, quick and painless, the way the Chinese do, and then I saw the empty slit in his collar. That did it; that did me in. I saw the slit and a chill began to rise in me, starting at my ankles and climbing me. I felt the skin over my old stab wounds begin to crawl, then a quick shiver like an electric shock raced through me, cracking like a whip along my spine. The pistol wobbled against his neck, nearly tumbling from my fingers.

God, the cowboy was fast. He only needed that one second. I didn't even see him whip around. I didn't see his hand when he stuck me in the thigh, high up by the pocket and hard into the bone where it wouldn't come out. I didn't see any of that, but I heard the nine snapping in my hand and then a howl and the sound of him running off into the desert. I dropped the gun into the dust and fell to the ground next to it. I curled up with my hands over my eyes, the handle of the knife prodding my belly.

After a while I pulled my hands from my face and they stuck a little, coming away with a damp and sour smell. I could see the glowing outline of the truck through a pale light coming from the east. It was the moon rising over the desert, liquid and slow and steady. From far off I heard the boy calling for me, but a wind had come up, and he seemed to be crying; the sound rose and fell, rose and fell.

Hold on, I yelled to him, *I'm coming*. Out on the road a semi-truck moaned past, eighty, ninety, and like an answer let off its horn, long and low. I felt around in the dust with my hand, my fingers found the gun; I closed my eyes and let the current take me out to him.

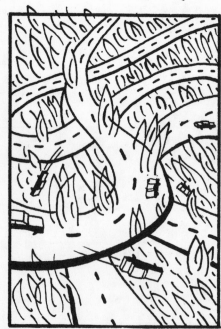

IN NEW JERSEY HIGHWAYS
BURST INTO FLAMES.

WHILE IN WASHINGTON TWO
MOONS ROSE IN DAYLIGHT.

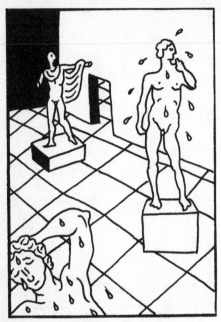

IN MUSEUMS STATUES
BEGAN TO SWEAT.

WHILE IN DENVER PEOPLE
GREW WOOL.

IN WISCONSIN CALVES WERE
BORN WITH SEVEN LEGS,

AND IN SAN FRANCISCO IT
RAINED RED HOT STONES.

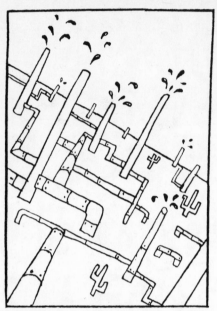

IN NEW MEXICO OIL
REFINERIES SPOUTED BLOOD.

AND IN BOISE PEOPLE WOKE FROM
DREAMS TO BE IN NIGHTMARES.

IN DETROIT POLICE
BECAME HENS,

AND HENS BECAME
POLICE.

IN MINNEAPOLIS PIGEONS
FELL LIKE RAIN.

AND IN MISSISSIPPI FIRES
WERE SEEN IN THE SKY.

IN ARKANSAS PEOPLE
FLOATED INTO THE AIR,

AND IN NEW YORK BUILDINGS
SHRANK TO THE SIZE OF APPLES.

IN ST. LOUIS WHEELS DROVE WITHOUT CARS,

WHILE IN SEATTLE REACTORS MELTED TO CHINA.

IN WYOMING, ASSEMBLY LINES DISASSEMBLED.

WHILE THE CITY OF ST. PAUL DISAPPEARED IN A PLUME OF SMOKE.

IN THE SKY ABOVE THE SUN APPEARED LOCKED IN COMBAT WITH THE MOON.

I WAS CALM SINCE KEITH AND KELLY OF NBC NEWS SAID THERE WAS NO NEED TO WORRY.

THE T.V. TURNED INTO A HEN AND RAN AROUND THE ROOM LAYING STONE EGGS.

THEN I BEGAN TO PANIC.

Nevertheless

I've never seen such a small child with a cast on her arm; Chana is only two. Still, she's just learned to drink from a cup and does not intend to let a broken arm stop her. Since she's too little to grasp a cup one-handed, she sips orange juice from a crystal shot glass, which Marlene, her mother, refills after every few swallows. Marlene is white with fatigue, and I'd worry about her even if she wasn't the daughter-in-law of my sweetheart, Paige, who will be back from the printer soon with leaflets for tomorrow's demonstration. I am on the floor. Marlene sets down the juice, kneels at my shoulders, and prepares to trace me onto a sheet of corrugated cardboard. She says, "Dean, a little animation. Please." But I am sixty-three years old, and not about to start now.

Tomorrow will be the fortieth anniversary of the bombing of Hiroshima, and perhaps a hundred of us will march on the air force base. This first year of Reagan's second term, the need seems particularly clear. The organizing committee, led by Paige and Marlene, has decided to make dozens of human silhouettes in black-painted cardboard and hang them on the base's chain link fence. Leaflets will explain that these represent shadows scorched onto rocks and walls by the blast. Only black shapes remain of people who, a moment before, had been shopping, strolling, attempting life's business. I'd often heard this story, but never from a primary source, and as a historian, I remain skeptical.

There's a stack of shadows in the corner: friends and neighbors of all sizes and shapes. Even Dunk, the Irish setter, was held down and traced by main force; his shadow resembles a huge, squashed frog. Marlene is represented clutching her head, and her husband, Paige's son Lou, makes a particularly striking effect: his left leg was amputated last spring. This is a family things happen to. I've pulled out Paige's shadow twice to admire it: fragile, big-bottomed, she's shaped like an inverted goblet. The figures are running, writhing, lying crumpled, and Marlene wishes I'd look more tormented. What breath she has—as if she ate nothing but flowers and chewing gum.

It's seven-thirty in the morning. I was up before dawn as always and made piles of pancakes and scrambled eggs, a gallon of Morning Thunder tea, and now the army of young peaceniks rushing through the big house is full of my food. I'm absurdly proud of this, just as I was sharply, perilously happy this morning to wash and tiptoe downstairs in the chill, leaving Paige asleep in the warm bed. Tormented? I hitch my legs sideways and turn my head. Marlene is not convinced.

The cast on Chana's tiny arm impresses me: It's not plaster, but a porous plastic tape that seems light and comfortable. At a picnic last month, Chana had been told to stick close to a twelve-year-old neighbor boy, who was flying an elaborate, winged box kite with vast, leering eyes. Everyone—I was not with Paige then—watched the kite climb through the boy's fingers to a height of hundreds of feet, tugging at two-hundred-pound test fishing line meant to weather any wind. Then they turned away, and drank and ate until a small plane, flying low, cut across the kite's string and jerked the boy ten feet into the air. Chana, clutching his leg, rose with him. Afterward, she told her mother, "You told me to take care!" She felt she'd been appointed the boy's guardian. He's out back now, still swaggering over his dislocated shoulder, and I doubt he knows Chana meant to save him.

At the end of the demonstration, a dozen of us will climb the fence into the base and be arrested. I will not be among them. Concerned for my career, Paige has asked me not to, and who would oppose her without good cause? She's one of those women of whom everyone says: How strong she is! Losing her husband to a younger woman, then nursing her son through cancer! People say the same of me: my wife passed twenty-three months ago. What a household! The divorcée, her amputee son, her ancient, widower boyfriend, the infant with the broken arm. I lie on the floor, well rested and full of warm tea. "Anguish," Marlene says, and I stick out an arm.

"Dean," she says patiently, "you're walking down your street. The one you grew up on. And this huge ball of fire blows up through the middle of it, and knocks down all the buildings, and kills all your friends, and is going to kill you, too, and end your whole world. How are you going to meet it?"

"Like this," I say and, straightening, lace my fingers neatly over my stomach. "Just like this."

After a moment, she nods. Planting her hand on my chest, she leans over me and starts to trace. Paige walks in, dewy with early heat. "Someone young will have to carry those boxes from the truck." She looks down at us and says, "Aha!"

Chana runs to meet her grandmother, almost stepping on my head. Close to my eyes, her tiny feet hang a long instant in midair.

What is it about laundromats that makes all their clients seem sallow, furtive, beaten, losers in general? I believe the effect is more pronounced at our age. My washing machine finally quit last spring, and a laundromat is where I met

Paige—or rather, first spoke to her at length—and it shocked me to see her there. I'd heard of the divorce, but I still pictured her as a faculty wife, someone with a crumbling, artfully furnished house of her own. Like mine. But there we were, lugging sacks of soiled clothes through that hideous, wax yellow light. We greeted each other by name. I should point out that she looked lovely and tired; it was I who felt sallow and shabby.

She said, "Did I mention I was living with my son? And his wife. It would be too *suburban* to get a washer and dryer of our own. Lord knows there's room."

"I have quite a big house myself."

"*Yes*." She was remembering Angie was dead. "Dean, I *am* sorry. I don't think I ever got a chance to say."

I lifted my hands. "Thank you."

We discussed weather, university news, and baseball, in which we both have a desultory interest. We leaned across a row of machines—leaning on one elbow is very rakish stuff for me—in the diaperish damp. "You are a very beautiful woman. I hope it's all right for me to say that."

"An old woman."

"No."

"Getting there."

Well, what of it? I suppose I should have contradicted her again. In any case, out came our photos. Paige said, "Now *there's* a good-looking woman. Your daughter?"

"No. That's Angie at forty-three." I was surprised. Not everyone agreed that my wife was beautiful. I showed Paige our daughter, who looks like me, poor girl.

She showed me her son Lou: long-haired, one-legged, with a seamed, smiling face. "Doesn't he look like hell? Well, he's alive." She told me the story of the cancer, of how Marlene, busy with one of her depressions, found it needful to take the infant Chana and leave for months, how Paige had moved in to nurse him. "She leads him a merry dance," Paige said. "Still gone the week he came back from the hospital, Lou slipped into a fever in the middle of the night. He thought his bed was full of cancer. An actual pool of it." In his delirium, Lou saw the cancer as a flood of glistening black curds, swarming up his remaining leg, covering his belly, his mouth. He knew he was about to slip under the foul mass and drown. His head and torso weighed thousands of pounds. He could not sit up. Paige got into bed with him and held him upright until he slept. "He did weigh a ton," she said. "Jesus, what *awful* things to say to a near stranger. Well, perhaps you won't stay a stranger." A machine went into the spin cycle, shaking our hips.

"My house is just a block away. Perhaps you'd like to come for coffee."

"Perhaps I would." When her machine stopped, she pulled out wet slacks and shook them. Drops of water spattered my cheeks, and she laughed. It took me a moment to want to wipe my face.

I will not be the one to say this, but it's an ugly dove; twice a man's height, lopsided, cartoony, almost hunchbacked. Like the shadows, it's made of painted corrugated cardboard, many sheets of it, representing months of scavenging for stove and refrigerator cartons. The law states we can use nothing stronger than cardboard tubes to brace it in back—nothing that might, say, be used as a club—and so after an hour of work, the big dove will not stand. Grunting, one-legged Lou hauls himself back into his wheelchair and says, "We need wood."

Marlene shakes her head slowly, gentling a severed wing. "I don't know. They say they're going back five years for priors on this one, and actions at other bases count. I've got to be back at work Wednesday. The latest. I mean, it's just a job, but those're getting hard to find." She and Lou will climb the fence. Over the last five years, Marlene's spent perhaps nine months in jail for protests like this one and is now concerned with serious time.

"They're not jerks," Lou says. "They want this quick and painless. Paige?" he calls. Beyond the splayed tail, Paige and a young woman are cross-legged on the kitchen linoleum, encircled by clipboards and neat stacks of paper. The phone is at Paige's hip. The entire business of this demonstration seems conducted by women sitting tailor-fashion on the floor while stiff-legged males shift from foot to foot.

Though she has not seemed to listen, Paige says, "There's some kind of do at the base at two-thirty, and the CO's hinted that if we're out by then, no surprises, we'll just get ban-and-bar letters. Get some of those wooden laths by the carport and slip them inside the tubes. They're not going to give this bird a physical. Lou, I'd rather you worked on the press sheet. QuikCopy closes at five."

Marlene lopes out for wood. Lou rolls to the desk and boots up the computer, an old Amiga that coughs and gurgles for minutes. He says, "Dean? Check my grammar?" Chana stumps importantly into the room, stares at the dove, gives it a judicious kick with her white sneaker, leaving no mark. She claws at Lou's knee until he scoops her into the empty space where his left thigh was. He says, "I'm working, Chugboat, so you be real good or you're out of here."

"Want to do the *bell*."

"That's the typewriter, Chug. This is the word processor."

"I'd be happy to take over, if you're busy," I say. I stand at his back, greedily close to them, reading over his shoulder. God help me, the boy's illiterate. These days, they all are.

Lou grins. "Dean, we don't have time for anything that good. If you could just catch my bigger bloopers."

I say, "This is needlessly inflammatory. I was a member of the armed forces myself, and I can assure you the rank and file is far from sinister." Lou cranks around, startled. "Yes. I feel like a bit of an imposter among you people. An ex-soldier." Paige patters in.

"That's *right!*" she says. "Dean, how terrific! You still have your old uniform, right?"

"Oh, now," I say.

Lou nods. "That's good. Any medals?"

"I was a supply sergeant. A great deal of power there, but very little glory. Let's see. A marksman's. A good conduct. Campaign ribbons. The same nonsense as everyone else."

"Beautiful," Lou says.

"Oh, now." The back door springs open, and Marlene enters with a cross-cut saw and the wood, preceded by the wobbling end of the long lath and followed by Dunk, who gallops through the closing door, tongue swinging.

Lou says, "Marlene, Dean was in the army. We're going to have him up front with the dove, wearing all his medals."

Marlene says, "Huh. Well. I guess you were young then. Keep that fucking dog off the *dove!*" But Dunk has already left three paw prints on its white cardboard breast—sharp, clear, heading straight up.

I could tell by the way Paige moved around my bookshelves that she was used to sizing up a library, and sure enough, I found she came to the university as an adjunct lecturer in chemistry twenty-seven years ago. "Just before I married The Prick." She had two sons immediately. When she returned to the university after the divorce, it was as a lab technician. By then, of course, her education was obsolete.

Flowered pillowcases full of her laundry slouched in a corner. I asked her to sit; I offered to warm up her coffee. I made a nuisance of myself.

She sat and asked, "What did your wife die of? Do you mind?"

I could see she knew I didn't mind. She knew I'd never be done talking about it.

"A number of things. Pneumonia, renal failure. She was nine years older, and never strong. She was no thicker through the chest than this book." I touched a dictionary on the table.

"Which of these books were hers?"

"The novels."

She kicked off her shoes and rested small stocking feet on the coffee table. "Do you mind?" she asked again.

"That etching was hers. That one with the cliffs."

"I think I've become morbid. There lately seem to be such strings of catastrophes."

"In the army, there was a general belief that a slight wound would exempt you from a severe one. One bullet per customer. I hate to think how often I saw that disproved."

"Were you wounded?"

"Not a scratch."

"Do you remember that girl who was pulled into the air by the kite? It was in the papers. That was my granddaughter." She told me the story: the slanting eyes of the kite, Chana riding the boy's leg into the air. No one could believe she was so strong. "Well, that's one thing we have in this family. Here, feel."

She took my hand and squeezed. She did not, in truth, have much of a grip. But her small hand was remarkably hard, like warm bone. And for a moment I felt, as perhaps I was meant to, that I was being drawn, in a modest way, into the air.

Marlene and Lou built the county's tallest house—four stories. Now their bedroom is behind the kitchen, and Lou's scarcely seen the top floor. The bottom three stories are populous: Lou's brother and sister-in-law (now finishing six-month terms for vandalizing warheads); a changing cast of engineering and science grad students who sometimes pay rent and sometimes don't; and Paige's suite, which, this weekend, she's sharing with me. And today the living room and kitchen swarm with young people working on tomorrow's protest. But nobody lives up here, where I now loaf and sightsee. The unused bathroom sparkles, and the curtainless windows open on miles of fields, which seem dusted with cinnamon. There has never been any furniture on these gleaming floors. Instead the rooms are filled with huge, hot-colored kites Lou made before his illness, including the leering one that pulled the children aloft. Lou tests the shattered vanes with his hands, stooping on his crutches, his shirt soaked with the effort of the climb. "It could be fixed, but . . . *ah*," he grins, pained.

We've stowed the completed dove up here in sections.

Lou says, "I asked Dad to show up tomorrow. Fat chance." He compresses his mouth and sends his eyebrows up. It's difficult to shrug on crutches. "Since I first went in, the poor shit can't look me in the eye. Like staying with Paige would've saved me. Christ, Marlene can't look me in the eye, either. All I want is someone to look me in the eye. Dean, look me in the eye.

"What are you staring at, old man?" he says, and laughs.

I run my hands along the windowsill. Real wood, smoothly mortised, a pleasure. Lou works in maintenance at the university and knows young people who know how to do things. To the south, the land is just creasing into the broad valley that will take it into the next state. Those low olive hills are over the line. We listen to the commotion downstairs. "I've met Dad's girlfriend," Lou says. "She's not bad. I mean, she's nearly forty. Everyone acts like he's dating some cheerleader."

"Your mother was a cheerleader."

"Maybe that's why she's so vicious about it. Now, me, I think it's best. This way. I'm glad Paige . . . I think she did okay for herself." I flush with pleasure.

"How much would you want to rent this top floor?" I say. But this is silly, random talk. Three flights of stairs! Still, my house in town is far too large.

"Oh, Dean. Take it slow, man."

And I remember my talk with Paige a week ago. She'd flushed as well. How pretty she looked! "Oh, Dean," she said, hugging my arm with both of hers. "I've *been* married."

Since Angie died, I hate to see a woman lying down when I'm standing, and the truth is, I wish Paige would get up off the bed. She's dressed to go out in stonewashed, pleated jeans and a blouse I like very much, shiny red with little matte red squares. There's nothing left to do for the rally, and soon it will be evening. Outside, light drains from the sky, the dim fields lift toward the purple clouds, or seem to, and the horizon retreats from us. Against this, the windowsill grows whiter, sharper, more domestic.

I can just hear Marlene's Volkswagen start up, and then Lou's truck. He screams, "Par*ty*! Par*ty*! Par*ty*!" Paige finally rises and takes my elbow. Outside, the warm front yard smells of wheat, of paint cans in the garbage, Lou's truck burning oil. Chained to a tree, Dunk yodels and sobs. Lou rolls down his window and says, "You old farts look better than I do."

It's night when we pull into the lot at Kumi's. Heat lightning dodges through the towering clouds, making them gleam from within. Kumi is the cook: Her husband, the ex-biker and ex-serviceman, lured her from an Osaka restaurant with the promise of her own place but still insists on handling the receipts himself. It's dark and stifling inside, and when the boy stamps our hands with Kumi's name, our sweat turns the Japanese character into more clouds. The roadhouse sprang up in the shell of a failed bowling alley. You can still see crude patches in the hardwood dance floor where they pried up the ball returns. The Linn Sisters band is playing, though no more than two sing at a time. The others dance with their friends and children until their turn comes around again.

We drag tables together and order pitchers of beer, baskets of tempura, platters of kappa maki. Marlene says, "Done. I can't believe we got it all done." Chana is dancing alone, flailing her good arm, and I remember how, asked to pose for her silhouette, she'd twisted herself happily into the postures of agonized death. The jigging farmers seem concerned about stepping on her. Some of the young organizers are dancing when the food arrives, but Paige and I and Lou, arms folded on his crutches, are waiting for the same thing: a slow number.

Marlene says, "You know, twice I've been out with Chana and people have tried to get her off to the side and find out if I beat her. I mean, that says something. That everybody would assume it's the mother if a child's hurt."

"I think it shows good concern," a young woman says.

Marlene crams her mouth with hummus and goes out to dance with Chana. "Uh, huh," Paige murmurs in my ear. "Now watch." Sure enough, within two minutes a young man has asked Marlene to dance, and she ruffles Chana's hair and goes off with him. Paige says, "It's only been thirty years. I haven't forgotten how it's done."

"Thirty years ago—" I realize, drunk on two beers.

"What?"

"You would never have looked at me."

"Quite likely not. My loss." She rests her chin on my shoulder. "You look very handsome tonight."

It has been some time since anyone bothered to lie to me about this.

Thirty years ago, I'd been married to Angie nine years.

Paige watches Marlene closely as she flickers through the crowd with a young man. "I'm to believe she just likes to dance more than Lou can," she says sourly. But Lou seems happy with his beer and his friends, and for the first time, I wish Paige would be quiet.

When our slow number arrives, Marlene is instantly at the table, and Lou is up before any of us. He squeezes her, growls happily. "This is what I deserve for living right." Then he pulls his baseball cap around backward and is ready to dance.

The girl now singing imagines that vibrato is an acceptable substitute for tunefulness. Out on the floor, I look down on the clean, white part in Paige's hair. There is still a measure of auburn among the gray, and I love both colors, though I'm wistful for the time she dyed it all to the same hue. But then we were married to other people. "I thought you said you didn't dance," she said.

"This isn't dancing. This is hugging."

Marlene leans into Lou as he rocks from crutch to crutch. Chana is trying to step on his moving shoe.

When a rock tune begins, we head toward the table, but Marlene snags my arm. "Come on, soldier. One more dance. Tomorrow we'll all be in jail. Paige, I'm stealing your man."

"Take him."

Marlene's breath is strong with garlic. She at once begins a complex and precise threshing motion, her narrow arms and hips weaving like the helical blades of an old-style push mower. Her dancing is the one thing I've seen her do that isn't slovenly, though her face is sullen as usual. Then she gives me a smile I haven't seen before, and tentatively, I begin to shuffle as the others do. Is it permitted to count time, even silently? I don't dance. Nevertheless, I'm dancing.

Lou's brother and sister-in-law will be out of jail early next month. They penetrated a cruise missile depot armed only with wire snips and Tupperware containers full of blood, which they managed to pour into three warheads, destroying them. The blood was their own; they'd been accumulating it for a year and had over a gallon. Lou himself, when he was a clean-cut twenty-one year old, donned a jacket to attend an open house at the General Dynamics Electric Boat facility. Slipping away from the crowd, he found a van with the keys in the ignition, locked himself inside, and rammed the hull of a new submarine until the van would no longer run. He served most of a one-year term. Marlene served four months for chaining herself to both halves of the main gate of a marine base, just before sunup. "You'll have to cut me in half if you want to do any business," she shouted. "Before you kill anyone else today, you'll have to kill me." Paige is new to civil disobedience, has never been in jail longer than overnight, and is unsure she has the nerve for longer terms. Meanwhile, she wants me kept out of it. I asked her, "What do you imagine the school can do to tenured faculty?"

"Anything they want," she assured me.

Now, seeing her sleep beside me, feeling the usual superiority of the last one awake, who watches over and protects, I'm reminded that Paige is far more likely to protect me.

Eyes closed, she says, "You're making quite a hit with Marlene."

Startled, I say, "Is it necessary, is there some *political* reason that girl must always look so . . . disheveled? She's got a little mustache. Wouldn't that be a simple thing to attend to?"

"Easy, boy."

"My daughter would give anything for a face like that." I touch Paige's chin, her cheek, with a careful thumb, which she turns and kisses. Then kisses me, and I can tell she means for us to sleep. I am either let down or relieved, but this in no way interferes with the kiss. There are by my count, eleven people in this big house tonight. All of us are healthy, and in the cupboards and refrigerators we have enough good food for weeks. None of us must sleep alone; even Chana has Dunk curled at her feet. None of us, unless our government intervenes, is likely to die by morning. This all seems remarkable. I watch Paige until I am almost certain she's asleep. I've never in my life seen a woman sleep on her side; Angie would just as soon have slept on her head. In the hospital, she'd insisted on her own nightgowns, some of them ten years old. Angie never wore out clothes. She insisted on having the blankets fixed as they were at home, and if not, she would neither sleep nor eat. Most of the nurses caught on, but there were always new ones, and more than once I came and remade her bed. I learned to do it as the nurses did, with Angie still in it.

"Don't fuss me," she'd whisper, after I made the fuss she required.

Needles had left a bruise like a black sun in the crook of her arm. A week later, she'd be buried with it.

"This will be getting cold." I set the tray back on her table. She tried a bit of apple cobbler and some tea.

"Muck," she said matter-of-factly. "Dean, why don't you have it? I'll bet you could use a little supper." At the end of this sentence, she was tired.

"You need to keep your strength up," I said, but she rucked her mouth down and gave me a fishy, disappointed eye, and that was the last dishonest thing I tried to say. She rapped the tray twice with a forefinger, and I took it and began. I was ravenous. She watched my mouth hungrily. When I was done, she didn't look hungry anymore. Her eyelids sank and she mumbled, and I smoothed her covers and made the folds even. I could not have lived with a woman for thirty-seven years who wasn't fussy. She mumbled again.

"What?"

I decided she wanted my hand. Anyway, she took it. She was very near sleep now. Her lips moved one more time.

"Dean," she said.

"I am right here," I said. "I will always be right here."

It is perfect weather, surprisingly temperate for August, and the dove looks, if possible, uglier than ever. We've punched holes in it to accommodate the breeze. Paige and I stand on either side, trying to keep it upright. How strong she is, people say, but physically she is quite fragile, and I wonder if she needs help. My uniform fits well, chiefly because I had a bit of a gut even at twenty. Could I really have enjoyed this stiff, drab cloth? Before us, a few photographers jockey for position, and behind us, the fence is festooned with black cardboard shadows, running, writhing, lying crumpled. Behind that, a young woman taking our pictures for the base files and the FBI, and military police in open vans. One calls, "Sir, I consider you a traitor to that uniform."

"Not an officer, son," I call back. "No need to 'sir' me."

"Sssshhh," Paige says.

"Air force twerps. They'd high-hat regular army no matter what."

Marlene has been addressing the crowd for some time in a clear, steady voice. She makes peace sound like something of a crackpot notion, I'm afraid. The twelve who will go over the fence stand in a row behind her: a young farming couple, some grad students, a few weather-beaten hippies, three plainclothes nuns, and Lou. The shadows dance cripple's dances as Marlene speaks again about Hiroshima, about the white flare erasing a city and etching its people into stone, about ten thousand flares unmaking the world. Lou watches her as if she's a pot about to boil over, absently stroking the hip above his stump. I can see he's feeling the phantom pain that never quite leaves him. He will roll under the fence instead of climbing it, while we haul up on the chain link. One of the young people has already scouted out a dip in the ground.

If I don't watch myself, I will doze. The truth is, I don't sleep at all well next to a strange woman. And as soon as I realize I've thought of Paige as a strange woman I turn to her, and so I miss the end of the speech, the twelve moving toward the fence, the first hand gripping the mesh as they begin to climb. A wind springs up and Paige's arms tremble. It's the historian's curse to wool-gather, and now I am months in the past. Again, Lou is home from the operation, home to his deserted house, feverish and shouting at midnight, sure that his bed is full of death and that he is headed under. Paige climbs in behind him, locks her arms around his ribs. "Hold on to me!" he screams. "I've got you," she says. "Hold on to me!" And she whispers—hisses—"*I am not going to let you go.*"

The Kid's Been Called Nigger Before

Toby sits in the back of the green Pinto wagon and sings until the windows fog up. He's got a dozen fresh batteries, four brand-new tapes, and the music's pumping loud through the headphones. Over the vibrating thrum of the engine, he tilts back his head and belts out a favorite line. A few more words, then he closes his eyes, the melody floating loose in his throat. Then he goes quiet, stroking his red hairpick in a steady four-four.

Marty lifts his eyes to the rearview mirror, then he smiles and shifts into third. Colleen is still filing her nails in silence beside him. She stops for a moment when Marty puts his hand on her knee, shakes her dark bangs from her eyes, then starts up with the file on her other hand. Marty looks from the mirror to her face. Toby picks up on a song behind them, following along in open-throated abandon. The car quivers for a moment in the pull of the storm front, and the wheels skate off toward the shoulder. Marty looks from the mirror to the road to Colleen, taking his hand from her knee, then he looks to the road again.

"That kid has got one set of lungs," he says.

Colleen sticks the file in the glove box, smacks it shut, then looks back at Toby. He's snapping his fingers and humming between his lips, low in his throat for the bass line, then switching to the melody in a whine through his nose. Toby's father is black, but her looks have come through in his cheekbones and the crossed overlap of his two front teeth. In the dwindling sunlight, his eyes are shot through with shards of green and his hair is a net of tangled curls.

"Like his father," she says to Marty, settling back in the seat and facing the windshield again.

"I guess," Marty replies, squinting into the oncoming traffic as he exits the interstate and merges with the two-lane highway. "But you're musical," he says. He remembers the first time she came to play at the Four Corners bar, where he drank every Saturday night. He'd been sitting at a table near the small red half-moon of carpeted stage, splitting pitchers of Stroh's with the boys from the bakery. They were waiting for Jonny "Love 'em and Leave 'em" Longnecker to walk out with his midnight-blue electric guitar and stand there in front of the shadows of his brother and his drum set. Jonny was local, twice divorced, drove a 1965 mint-condition red Mustang with a black leather top, and did the books for his family's excavating business. His brother, David—"Davey Jay"—Junior, was five years younger, and state certified in heavy equipment. Weekdays, the Longnecker brothers worked out of their green aluminum-sided garage west of town on Industrial Drive. Weekends, they made music at Four Corners, and had a way of getting both lucky and in trouble with women.

That evening, when the manager announced Jonny was down sick with the flu, the crowd had booed and hissed, lobbing peanut shells and·wadded-up cocktail napkins at the stage.

They were still making noise when Colleen walked out and adjusted the mike, planting her feet on the stage as her fingers trembled against the stand. She sat curled around her guitar on a stool for a moment, waiting for the crowd to settle down.

"This is a song about someone who used to love me," she said softly, without even introducing herself. Then she'd leaned forward and started to sing. By the end of her very first number, even the die-hard Jonny Longnecker fans had settled into listening, including the boys playing pool for serious money in the back. When she finished, they pounded their cues on the floor until she started up again.

She'd played three sets that night, and each song was a story of something she'd lived through. Just after midnight, one of the boys playing pool took off his Stetson, dropped a handful of quarters inside, then passed it to a nearby table. The hat made the rounds of the bar, and by one it was filled with dollar bills.

Nobody in the crowd knew much about Colleen, except that she worked the counter at some party store and wasn't local, but she was pulling stories from their lives as she sang about hers. Marty sat there that night studying how her hair had a way of falling forward, hiding half her face and making shadows across the top of her guitar. Every so often, though, she'd lift up her head for a moment, wincing as she lingered over certain phrases, then dropping back down again.

That's what he remembers as he turns on the headlights, saying, "And you're the one raising him, after all. He's your kid, too."

At home in the white clapboard rental house, it's just the three of them going through their lives together, and most of the time Colleen forgets Toby's half black. Then she's reminded, quickly, uncomfortably, at school carnivals and potlucks, or in lines at the IGA. People startle, turn away, then twist back in a slow double take. They look from her face to his, and don't even pretend not to gawk. Toby says he's used to it. He shakes it off, saying, "Never mind, what do they know?" When people nearby get to whispering and staring,

Colleen moves in close to her son and smiles like nothing is wrong. She puts her hand to his shoulder, though she knows she can't really protect him. Most people drop away once she's there close beside him with her smile in place, though every so often there are some who smile back and forth between their faces in a curious sort of compassion. "Your son has such beautiful eyes," they say brightly, or, "My, he's a tall one, all right."

She'd met his father over thirteen years back, a lifetime ago she tells Marty when they talk. Larry played drums, working as a studio musician when Motown was still in Detroit, and he sang in a sweet liquid tenor.

She'd been working at a record store in the city for ten months, moving from Saginaw to live in an apartment with her sister, Patti, and helping out with the rent. Her parents had said it was the least she could do, seeing as she wasn't working a real job. Playing guitar in a band at the bowling alley didn't count as regular employment, they informed her, and neither did holing up in her room all day writing lyrics in a notebook and practicing chords. On her twentieth birthday, her father came home from his job at the cement factory and handed her a Trailways ticket for Detroit. Two days later, he'd driven her downtown in his truck, loading her guitars and two suitcases onto the bus, the same as he'd done with Patti.

Her sister studied art at Wayne State, and modeled nude in the evenings for figure-drawing classes. That money was off the books, collected in an old coffee tin during class, and Patti laughed as she counted the money at night, spilling it out on her bedspread. "Wouldn't Daddy have a fit if he knew about this?" she giggled, but Colleen said she wasn't so sure he'd even care.

Neither of them had a car or more than a few dollars left after rent, even with the modeling money, but Patti got food stamps and managed to keep them fed. Patti had a skinny, red-haired boyfriend in the army, Terri Hawkins. They'd been high school sweethearts, and he'd given her a star-sapphire ring the night before he reported for basic. Ten months later, he got killed in Vietnam, somewhere near the Delta and eleven days short of coming home. Patti and Colleen had stood on the asphalt at Detroit Metro, in icy rain the week before Christmas, not quite believing that the gray military casket coming down from the belly of the plane was really Terri. Six soldiers in dress greens stood at attention on either side of the casket, and Patti waited there without moving or speaking as an officer saluted her, handing over an American flag and a small plastic bag of personal belongings.

The two of them sat up that night in their apartment, and drank a gallon of pink Chablis as they sorted through his things at the kitchen table. Other than his dog tags, there wasn't much to look over, just a daybook and photographs, pictures of the men in his unit—dirty and anxious-faced boys hamming it up in the jungle sun, boys in government-issue T-shirts and fatigue pants staring into the camera, the last people to see Terri alive. Patti put the pictures in her jewelry box, along with a letter that had never been finished, her name and Terri's looped together at the top of page one in a circle of penciled hearts. "Dearest Patti Cakes," it began. "Sarge sent the papers to the chaplain. If we meet at Fort Bragg, they can get us married in a week." The next morning, they smoked a joint to take the edge off their headaches, and followed the hearse along the interstate to Saginaw.

The army had sealed the casket, saying that's how they handled those things. Mrs. Hawkins had thrown a fit at the funeral home, insisting she be allowed to view the remains of her oldest son, arguing that no one would ever know if that was really her Terri in there. The Methodist minister followed her into the bright lights of the room in the funeral home basement. Later he'd stood with his arm around her shoulders as she greeted people in the parlor during visitation, white-faced over what she had seen. Patti told Colleen that she didn't need to see anything more than what she'd found in the bag of his belongings.

They went back to their apartment after Christmas, and Patti hung her ring in the middle of Terri's dog tags around her neck. After that she stayed stoned and quit eating. Sometimes she'd sit at the kitchen table with the metal tags pressed between her lips as she studied her art books and sorted seeds from a bag of dope. Colleen wrote a song about that. She'd never had anyone to write about before. Except herself.

She'd met Larry two weeks after the funeral, coming into the record store during a January blizzard. He wore a black leather jacket and a black wool beret. He spent two hours bent over the record bins, holding albums up to his face and reading the credits on the jackets. Then he came up to Colleen at the counter.

"You cut me a deal on these records, I'll take you to dinner."

She studied the length of his fingers as he drummed on the glass counter-top. "I don't cut deals for anyone," she said. Then she looked up at him. His eyes seemed to fill half his face. They were perfectly round and his lashes were as long as a girl's.

"Well, then just dinner."

The next day, Patti said, "Don't go bringing that nigger around here."

"Black," Colleen said. "The word is 'black.' "

"The word's 'nigger' in my house," she corrected, fingering the silver tags which hung against her heart. "And how come he didn't get sent half the world away to die?"

One week later, the two of them found a place of their own, and Larry stayed home and wrote songs while she worked in the record store. He even wrote a song for her once, banging it out on the old piano they'd traded her twelve-string guitar for, working on the melody in their apartment off Inkster and Eight Mile. She hadn't liked the lines he put in about the color of her eyes, but she never let him know, since he'd started insisting she was unnaturally suspicious. Those days she showed up at the studio, he said he could just feel the heat rising between her and his girls singing backup. Then she got pregnant and every few nights he stayed out until dawn. Then Toby was born and he stopped coming home at all.

In the car now, she tosses her head side to side, fingering the pulse at her temples. She'd thought she'd forgotten all that. The car shimmies in the wind, and she looks over at Marty, at his tall slender body, and her heart starts winding back down. The first time he kissed her he'd put his hands to her face, then pulled back her hair from her eyes. He's got silky blond hair, baby-fine and hanging forward over his high freckled forehead. The heater's not working right, and he's zipped up his navy-blue parka to his chin.

"Hi, stranger," he says. "Where you been?"

"Thinking," she says. "But I'm back."

Marty likes old songs, songs he knows the words to, but he tells her he can listen to just about anything. He bought her a stereo and says he's ignorant about music in general, telling her he doesn't mind listening to love songs by black men, if that's what she likes. Those are the songs she plays when she gets into one of her moods, songs sung by men who can't let go, give up, figure out, deny or withhold all the loving they're feeling for someone. Or some other somebody else.

Toby rewinds a tape in the backseat, punching buttons, muttering, "Nope, nope," then hissing out, "Yes," and he starts to hum. He likes it when his mother sings. He likes how she puts songs on the stereo when Marty leaves for work, watching through the living room window as he backs out the drive. She stands at the window, singing every word perfect as Marty heads down the road into town for the night shift at Wonder bread, her hips swaying under her nightgown and an arm at her waist. She holds a hand to her shoulder and turns and swirls across the carpet, slow dancing all alone, not the way she has to move with Marty, who says his feet are too dumb to dance and makes them all laugh.

Toby clears the fog from the window on his left and looks west to the tree line. They're thirty-two miles from their home in the middle of Michigan. His father sent him a Walkman UPS from Los Angeles for Christmas. He called Christmas evening and asked Toby to come out to visit, saying, "You grown now, boy. Ought to let your old man have a look-see." But his mother said L.A. was no place for a twelve-year-old kid. Toby wants to go just to know what it's like, to meet the musicians his father works with, not to stay, he told his mother. To visit. He looks back at the trees where the sun is setting, wide currents of red running through the dark bank of clouds. The wind brushes sheets of snow over the stubbled fields, and he breaks into singing again.

"You okay?" Marty asks, reaching over to touch Colleen's cheek, and she nods, pulling at the threads of a button hanging loose on the front of her coat. "Look at the sunset," he says, and she turns to the window beside him.

Marty stares at her then, her face taking on pink in the light rising up from the horizon. Then he turns back to the road, drawing away from the center line.

"Hey, listen," he says. "Don't worry about that stuff with Dad. He's worked his whole life for Oldsmobile. That's where he gets that stuff about Toby. He's old. And he's mean when he drinks. I'm still glad we went. After all, how long we been together? A year now? And I'm glad that he met you, and Toby took it well, at least as well as he could. He's a good kid, you know."

"I should have let your old man have it," Colleen says, low and quick. "I should have given him a piece of my mind." Then she pauses, tightening her eyes in a squint. She'd put off meeting Marty's family as long as possible. He'd been asking for months, saying they could just drive down to Lansing, meet the old man, meet his family, get it over with. She had known it would go like this. "No," she says slowly, drawing the word out. "I should have punched him in the nose."

At eleven that morning, Marty's mother had met them at the door of the square pink-brick house with green trim. She'd come out on the porch when they pulled in the yard, her lips lifting high above her dentures. She'd hugged Marty and Colleen, then pulled back uncertainly as Toby extended his hand. Colleen held her breath for a moment, then broke loose with a smile as Marty's mother grabbed Toby's hand and pulled him close.

"You like turkey, young man?" she asked, and Toby grinned at the ground, nodding as she patted his head.

Once inside the door, Marty's mother got busy hanging up their coats, talking and laughing at nothing as they walked down the short narrow hall-way to the living room. Marty's father sat watching television on a sofa by the window that faced the front yard. He looked up only once as they entered the room, then stood and walked past them without saying a word. Colleen stepped back through the doorway, watching as he pulled on a heavy wool coat in the kitchen at the end of the hall. Then he pulled on his gloves and went out to his woodpile in the back of the house, splitting logs until the meal was laid out on the table.

Rhonda, Marty's sister, wheeled into the yard around noon in an old blue Impala. The backseat was hopping with her kids, an eight-year-old girl with brown pigtails sticking out above her ears, a ten-year-old boy with a broken tooth, and a baby in a yellow snowsuit she pulled free from the car and bounced up on her hip. They came busting into the house, loud and cold and hungry, Rhonda wobbling on high heels, swaying with the weight of the baby, her skinny bare legs pimpled with cold down past her knee-length leather coat, rolling her red-rimmed eyes.

"Darryl's too hung over to make it," she said, holding a cigarette between the tips of her red nails. She took off her coat in the living room, saying, "Men, we'd be better off without them most the time." She held her cigarette in one hand, and then held out the other to Colleen. "And I'm Rhonda," she said, "seeing as nobody around here knows enough to introduce us." Then her voice trailed off as she followed her kids to the kitchen, asking, "What's Daddy doing chopping wood out there in this kind of weather anyway?"

Marty's mother set up a little television in the kitchen so the children could watch the New Year's parades. Toby played on the floor with Rhonda's baby girl, making a game out of rolling a blue rubber ball into an empty Cheerios box. Colleen peeled potatoes and yams with the women and listened to the sound of the ax splitting logs in the yard.

Toby turns off the tape and slips off the headphones, then looks out the window again. It's dusk and it's started to snow. Large star-shaped flakes float sleepily through the twilight. He writes his name on the window, then adds "nigger" beside it, and pulls up his hands in the sleeves of his coat. He studies the back of Marty's head, the headlights of the oncoming cars catching the loose hair at Marty's shoulder in a white glow. In the future, he imagines Marty might look like the man he met today: old, grizzled, a hearing aid plugged into each furry ear. Toby's grown used to Marty, to the odd nervous way he drives, how he teases him about girls now, and he likes how he's sweet on his mother. When Marty stood up at the table and shouted at his own father, "You son of a bitch," Toby'd gone all cold inside.

"Marty," Toby said as they loaded themselves back in the car. "Don't worry about the kid. The kid's been called nigger before."

"That doesn't make it right," Marty answered, turning the key in the ignition and fluttering the gas pedal as the engine squealed and caught. "Does it?" he said, so loud and mad that Toby just sat there in silence.

From the moment they started dinner, Marty's father had sat at the table and studied Toby, staring first at him, then staring at his mother. He'd stop to take a bite of food from his plate, then start looking back and forth again, chewing slowly and breathing hard through his nose. Halfway through the meal, his mother put her fork down, then folded her hands in her lap.

"Excuse me," she said to Marty's father. "Would you mind explaining why you need to keep staring at me and my son?" The old man sat there slicing turkey on his plate for a good full minute, then he lifted up his face.

"Lady," he said then. "You got a nigger for a son," and everyone stopped eating.

Toby'd been called nigger before, but when the old man spit out that word, he couldn't do a thing except sit there and stare at his plate. His mother sat in the chair beside him for a moment, then she'd stood and put her hand on his shoulder. Marty rose from the table a second later, yelling at his father, then the three of them put on their coats. His mother had gone pale, begging a cigarette off Rhonda before they walked out to the car, even though she'd quit smoking two years back.

The heater fan's busted and Marty flexes the ache of his fingers against the wheel. When they get to the house, he'll build a fire in the wood stove and play video games with Toby. He bought the Nintendo for Christmas, for all of them, he'd said, saying he'd always wanted one, but really, he wanted it for the kid. Colleen had been complaining about Toby going downtown to the arcade, spending his quarters in the game machines. She worried that someone would get him, someone who hung out in places like that, looking for boys.

Colleen wraps her coat around her, turns up the collar, then says, "I really wouldn't have punched your old man." His father had frightened her, and that made her mad. She doesn't like being scared. She's worried that Marty will look at her differently now, that he won't like Toby so much anymore, and that someday he'll start feeling like he's in too deep, that he'll get an itch and take off. "I'm used to being alone," she says.

Toby leans forward between the two bucket seats, the headphones circling his neck. "I'm sorry I ruined the day."

"What do you mean, 'being alone'?" Marty asks.

"You didn't ruin the day," Colleen says to her son. "I mean how it was before you," she tells Marty. "When I lived all alone for ten years with my kid. That's what I mean."

"I like how it is now," Toby says, his voice rising in a tremble. "I'm sorry I spoiled the day," he adds, sinking back in the seat.

"You *didn't* spoil the day!" Marty yells. "And I like it, too. I like how it is. Nothing is spoiled or ruined. Is it?" he says. "Is it?" he repeats, taking a left at the 7-Eleven.

"Just don't you turn out like your father," Colleen warns, and she feels her voice shaking and holds her purse tight in her lap. "Don't you ever call my kid nigger," she says, and she lets it out, her tears running hot down her cheeks.

Toby looks down the road in front of them. The snow is falling in heavy wet flakes in the headlights, slurring beneath the tires.

"Nigger," he says quietly.

Colleen lifts her head, shakes it in disbelief.

"Nigger," Toby repeats loudly. "Coon, spearchucker, junglebunny, Rastus, apeface, shithead nigger, asshole nigger, lazy nigger, dirty little nigger." Marty looks back over his shoulder, the car lurching once to the right, and the tires grate the shoulder. Toby leans forward, placing his head between theirs, taunting, "Nigger — nigger — nigger" in a school yard singsong.

"Toby," Colleen scolds in a whisper.

Toby gives a whoop and leans back in the seat. "That's all, folks," he says. Marty starts to smile, and he looks at Colleen. She's holding her fingers to her lips. Then she leans sideways and falls against him, lifting her hands from her face.

The wiper blades move slowly with the weight of the snow, cutting two perfect arches against the glass. Colleen drops her head on Marty's shoulder, and he ropes his arm around her neck to pull her close. Her hair bobs in a cushion at his chin as she laughs, her voice rising up in a thin loose music he can barely hear.

Anodyne

My mother began going to gun classes in February. She quit the yoga. As I understand it, yoga is concentration. You choose an object of attention and you concentrate on it. It can be, but doesn't have to be, the deity. This is how I understood it. The deity is different now than it used to be, it can be anything, anything at all pretty much. But even so, my mother stopped the yoga and went on to what is called a "thirty-eight"—a little black gun with a long barrel—at a pistol range in the city. Classes were Tuesday and Thursday evenings from five to seven. That was an hour and a half of class and a half hour of shooting time. I would go with her and afterward we would go to the Arizona Inn and have tea and share a club sandwich. Then we would go home, which was just the way we left it. The dogs were there and the sugar machine was in the corner. We left it out because we had to use it twice a day. My mother and I both had diabetes and that is something you can not be cured of, not ever. In another corner was the Christmas tree. We liked to keep it up. Although we had agreed not to replace any of the bulbs that burned out. At the same time we were not waiting until every bulb went dark before we took the tree down either. We were going to be flexible about it, not superstitious. My grandmother had twelve orange juice glasses. A gypsy told her fortune and said that she would live until the last of the twelve glasses broke. The gypsy had no way of knowing that my grandmother had twelve orange juice glasses! When I knew my grandmother, she had seven left. She had four left when she died. The longest my mother and I ever kept the tree up was Easter once when it came early.

This is Tucson, Arizona, the desert floor. Around us are mountains, and one mountain is so high there is snow in the winter. People drive up and make snowmen and put them in the back of their trucks and on the hood of their cars and drive back down again, seeing how long they will last. My mother and I have done that, made a little snowman and put him on the roof of the car. There are animals that live up there who do not know the animals below them in the desert exist. They might as well be in different galaxies even though the difference is only a few thousand feet in elevation. Numbers interest me and have since the second grade. My father weighed one hundred pounds when he died. Each foot of a saguaro cactus weighs one hundred pounds. My father weighed no more than one cactus foot. I weigh seventy-two pounds, my mother weighs one hundred twenty, the dogs weigh eighty each. Our Buick station wagon weighs more than two tons. I do my mother's checkbook. Each month, according to the bank, I am accurate to the penny. We have enough money, not a great deal, but enough.

The man who taught the class and owned the firing range was called the Marksman. He called his business an Institute. The Pistol Institute. There were five people attending the class in addition to my mother: three women and two men. They did not speak to one another; no one wanted to make friends. They did not exchange names. My mother had a friend in yoga class, Suzanne. She was disturbed that my mother had dropped the yoga and was going to the Institute, and she said that she was going to throw the *I Ching* and find out what it was, exactly, my mother thought she was doing. If she did, we never heard the results.

My mother was not the kind of person who lived each day and objected to it, day after day. She was not. And I do not mean to suggest that the sugar machine was as large as the Christmas tree. It is about the size of my father's wallet which my mother now uses as her own.

When my father died my mother felt that it was important that I not suffer a failure to recover from his death and she took me to a psychiatrist. I was supposed to have twenty-five minutes a week with the psychiatrist, but I never had twenty-five minutes. It was more than fifteen, but not much more. Once, he used some of that time to tell me that he was dyslexic and that the beauty of words meant nothing to him, nothing, but that he appreciated their meaning, even enjoyed their meaning. I told him that one of our dogs is epileptic and that I had read about epilepsy and how in the first moments of an epileptic attack some people felt such a happiness they would be willing to give up their lives to keep it and he said that he doubted a dog would want to give up its life for happiness. I told him that dead people are very disappointed when you visit them and they discover you are still flesh and blood, that they are not angry but sad. He dismissed this completely. He did not comment on this or make a note of it. I suppose he's used to people trying things out on him.

My mother did not confide in me but I felt she was unhappy that February. We stopped the ritual of giving each other our needles in the morning before breakfast. I now gave myself my injections and she her own. I wanted it the other way, I missed the other way, but she had changed the policy and that was that. She still kissed me good morning and good night and took the dogs for long walks in the desert and fed the wild birds. I told her I had read that you should not feed the birds in winter, that it fattened up the wrong kind of bird or something. The good birds left and came back, left and came back, but the bad ones stayed and were strengthened by the habits of people like my mother. She said she didn't care. I told her this, I think, to be unpleasant because I missed the needles together but it didn't matter; she had changed her policy about the needles but not the birds.

The Pistol Institute was in a shopping mall where all the other buildings were empty and for lease. It had glass all across the front and you could see into it, the little round tables where people sat and watched the shooters and the long display case where the guns were waiting for someone to know them, to want them. When you were inside, you could not see out, the glass was dark. It seemed to me the reverse of what it should be but it was the Marksman's place, it was his decision. Off to the right as you entered was the classroom and over its door was the sign IF YE WILL BE SHEEP YE WILL BECOME MUTTON. No one asked what this meant, to my knowledge. I would not ask. I did not ask questions. I had started off doing this deliberately some time before but now I did it naturally. Off to the left behind a wall of clear glass was the firing range. The shooters wore ear protectors and stood at an angle in little compartments firing at targets on wires that could be brought up close or sent further away by pressing a button. The target showed the torso of a man with large square shoulders and a large square head. In the left-hand corner of the target was a box with the same figure much reduced. This was the area you wanted to hit when you were good. It was not tedious to watch the shooters but it was not that interesting either. I preferred to sit as near as possible to the closed door of the classroom and listen to the Marksman speak.

The Marksman stressed awareness and responsibility. He stressed the importance of accuracy and power and speed and commitment and attitude. He said that having a gun was like having a pet or having a child. He said that there was nothing embarrassing about carrying a gun into public places. You can carry a weapon into any establishment except those that serve liquor unless you're requested not to by the operator of that establishment. No one else can tell you, only the operator. Embarrassment is not carrying a gun, the Marksman said. Embarrassment is being a victim, naked, in a bloody lump, looked upon by strangers. That's embarrassment, the Marksman said.

The Marksman told horrible stories about individuals and their unexpected fates. He told stories about doors that were opened a crack when they had been closed before. He told stories about tailgating vehicles. He told a story about the minivan mugger, the man who hid under cars and slashed women's Achilles tendons so they couldn't run away. The Marksman said, "Be aware of who can do unto you." He said the attitude you have toward others is important. Do not give them the benefit of the doubt. Do not give them the benefit of the doubt or you could already be dead or dying. The distinction between dead and dying was an awful one and I would often have to go into the bathroom, the one marked DOES, and wash my hands and dry them, holding and turning them for a long time under the hot air dryer.

The Marksman told the story about the barefoot, bare-chested madman with the machete on the steps of the capitol in Phoenix. This was the Marksman's favorite story, illustrating as it did the difference between killing power and stopping power. The madman strode forward for sixteen seconds after he had been warned and his chest blown out. You could see daylight through his chest. You could see the gum wrappers on the marble steps behind him right through his chest. But for sixteen seconds he kept coming, wielding his machete and in those sixteen seconds he annihilated four individuals. My mother kept taking the classes and I heard this story more than once.

My mother decided that she wanted to know the Marksman socially and she invited him to dinner along with the others in the class. We decided on a buffet-style arrangement, the plates and silverware stacked off to the side. This way, if no one came, we would not feel humiliated. The table had not been set. No one came except the Marksman. Not the fat lady, who had her own pistol and her own purple holster for it, not the bald man or the two college girls, not the other man with the tattoo of a heron on his arm. The Marksman was a thin man in tight clothes wearing a gold chain and a small mustache. Sometimes he favored bloused shirts but that night he was wearing a jacket. I sat with him in the living room while my mother was in the kitchen. The dogs came in and looked at him. Then they jumped onto the sofa and curled up and looked at him.

"You allow those dogs every license, I see," he said.

I said nothing. I wanted to say something but I had no idea what it was. He asked me if I'd been to Disneyland.

"No," I said.

"How about the other one, the one in Florida?"

I said that I hadn't.

Where are you from, he asked me, and I said, here.

"I'm from San Antonio," he said. "Have you ever been to San Antonio?"

"No," I said.

"There's a big river there, a big attraction that runs right through the city past shops and restaurants and it's all lit up with fairy lights," the Marksman said. "Tourists take cruises on it and stroll beside it. They promenade," he said in a careful voice. "Once a year, they pump the whole thing out, the whole damn river, and clean it and then put the water back in again. They scrub the bottom as though it were a bathtub and fill it up again, what do you think about that?"

My hands were damp. I was beginning to worry about this. My mother always said there was nothing more useless than dreading something you weren't understanding.

"People have lost their interest in reality," the Marksman said.

My mother finally came back into the room with the salad and the bread. We made up our plates and sat down at the table. Sometimes we said grace; lately we had not been saying grace, but that evening my mother said in her high, hoarse voice, "Minds of murderers are easily divined but this though . . . death . . . the whole of death . . . to hold it all so gently and be good . . . this is beyond description. . . ."

It was like a grace, coming as it did before dinner. It was from somewhere but I had no idea where. I had my head bowed but my eyes were open. I had shut the dogs in my bedroom and I could see their black noses pressed against the bottom of the door where it did not meet the floor.

The Marksman said, a little insincerely I thought, "That's powerful." This did not diminish my opinion of him, however. My opinion, anyway, was not formed very well. We began to eat and then we had eaten and the Marksman went home.

The classes continued at the Institute. The old group left and a new one took their place. They had the same silent demeanor. It was like a technique. I stayed close to the door. The Marksman said never to point the muzzle of a gun at something you weren't willing to destroy. He said that often, with practice, you're just repeating a mistake. He stressed caution and respect. He stressed response readiness and alertness. He said you should always be in a state of heightened awareness, that it wasn't bad and it could save your life. When class was over, everyone and my mother filed out and chose their handgun and brought their box of ammunition and strode to their appointed cubicle.

My mother did not extend any more invitations to the group for dinner, although the Marksman came every Friday. It became the custom. I knew my mother did not exactly want him in our life, but she wanted him somehow. There are many people who have long artificial friendships like this, which become quite fulfilling, I'm sure. I tried to imagine him living with us. The used targets papering the shelves, his bloused shirts hanging on the clothesline, his enormous waxed black truck in the driveway. I imagined him trying to turn my father's room into a saferoom, for the Marksman spoke often about the necessity of a saferoom in a house, every house. The requirements were a solid core door, a dead bolt, a telephone, and a loaded gun, and it was the place where you should immediately go when a threat presented itself, a madman or a fiend or merely someone or something who, for whatever reason, wanted to kill you and cease your life forever. My father had died in his room but the way I understand it with very few modifications it could be made into a saferoom of the Marksman's specifications.

The psychiatrist had said that my father had been fortunate to have his room, in his own house with his own family, that is my mother and myself and the dogs. I don't know why he spoke to me in this way. He spoke to me in tiny measures. It was as though he were giving me tiny cups of water to swallow.

I liked the Marksman's truck. One Friday night when we were eating dinner I told him so.

"You're an American girl is why," the Marksman said. "Something in the American spirit likes great size and a failure to be subtle. Nothing satisfies this better than a truck."

The Marksman usually ignored me but he would address me if I spoke directly to him. With my mother, he was courteous. I think he liked her but didn't know how to go about things. She did not like him. I didn't know what she was doing. She had not become a very good shot either.

My mother and father loved one another. He had been a big strong man before he got sick. He had favorite things. He had favorite movies and meals and places. He had a favorite towel even. It was a towel I'd had with trains on it, big old-fashioned trains. He said he liked it because whichever way he dried himself he felt he was getting somewhere, but when he got sick he couldn't wash himself or dry himself or feed himself either. When he was very sick my mother had to be careful when she washed him or his skin would come off on the cloth. He liked to talk but then he grew too weak to talk. My mother said my father's mind was strong and healthy so we read to it and talked to it. I grew to hate the thought of it, this hidden mind in my father's body.

The Marksman had been coming over for several weeks when he appeared one evening with a cake in a box for dessert. I told him that we could not have dessert, that we had the sugar. It had never come up before.

"What do you do on your birthday without cake?" he said.

"I have cake on my birthday," I said.

He did not ask me when my birthday was.

I wanted to show him how I used the sugar machine, but I didn't want to tell him about it. I took the lancet, which was in a plastic cylinder and cocked with a spring, and I touched it against my finger to get a drop of blood. I squeezed the single drop onto the very center of the paper tab, onto a little circle there, and put it into the machine. My mother was outside, in the back of the house, putting out fruit for the birds, halves of oranges and apples. I looked at the screen of the machine, pretending more interest than

I actually had, as it counted down and then made the readout. One hundred twenty-four, it said.

"I'm all right," I said.

The Marksman just watched me. "You're an American girl," he said.

"What are you doing?" my mother said. We used the machine in the morning and the afternoon. We didn't use it at night.

"I'm all right," I said. "Nothing."

I took the pitcher of water off the dining table and busied myself by pouring some into the saucer of the Christmas tree stand. The tree wasn't taking water anymore. The room was sucking up the water, not the tree. Still it looked all right; it was still green.

"Do you want to learn to shoot?" the Marksman asked me.

"Goodness no," my mother said. "Isn't there a law against that or something? She's just a child."

"No law," the Marskman said. "The law allows you certain rights, you, me, her, everybody." I wondered if he was going to say I could be a natural but he didn't.

"No," my mother said. "Absolutely not."

I didn't say anything. I knew that I would not be with my mother always.

I went to the psychiatrist for a while longer. I went to him longer than my mother and I went to the Institute. We stopped going to the Institute and the Marksman stopped coming over for dinner. The last time I went to the psychiatrist there was a new girl in the waiting room. There had always been a little girl and one about my age and then this new one, an older one. We were all girls there. It was a coincidence, is my understanding, that there were no boys. The littlest one was cute, she had red hair and a pretty, heart-shaped mouth and she carried a toy, a pink-and-purple dinosaur. She was always trying to give it away. You could tell that she liked it, that she'd had it probably since she was born, it was all worn smooth and gnawed in spots. Once I got there and she had another toy, a rabbit wearing an apron, and I thought that someone had actually been awful enough to take the dinosaur when she offered it. But it showed up with her again and she was back to trying to give it to me and not just me but anyone who came into the waiting room. That seemed to be the little girl's problem, or one of them.

The new girl told us that she was there because her hair was thinning and making her ugly. It looked all right to me but she said that it was thinning and that she had to spend an hour each day lying upside down with her head on the floor to stimulate its growth. She said she had to keep the hairs in the brush and the hairs on her pillows. She said she'd left some hairs on a blouse she hadn't collected yet and her mother had taken the blouse and put it in the laundry and when she found out about it she had become so upset she had done something she didn't want to talk about. The other girl, the one my age, said our aim should be to get psychopharmacological treatment instead of psychotherapy, that this was what we should aim for, otherwise it was a waste of time, but this was what she always said.

I was the last of us to see the psychiatrist that afternoon. When my time was almost up he said, "You're a smart girl, tell me, which do you prefer, the manifest world or the unmanifest one?"

It was as though he were asking me which flavor of ice cream I liked. I thought a moment, then went to the dictionary he kept on a stand and looked the word up.

"The manifest one," I said, and there was not much he could do about that.

Children with Mantras

Three months after his father left, Daniel's mother took the family to learn transcendental meditation at the Lotus Flower Holistic Arts Center in Fishkill. She had heard about TM at a lecture given at the community college where she took night classes. The Maharishi himself did not appear, but was represented by a life-size photograph in the center of the stage. A dozen believers sat cross-legged around it, describing how transcendental meditation had changed their lives.

"For the first time since I was twelve, I don't have migraines," said a young man in glasses.

"My thyroid cancer is now in remission," said a woman with baby-fine hair, a pale scar on her throat.

The meditators talked about "focus" and "inner harmony." They described TM as a psychic vitamin that helped them dispel their anxieties. They were placid, almost vegetative with bliss, their faces as pearly as fresh cloves of garlic. Given the recent upheavals in her family, Daniel's mother did not think that this was such a bad way to be.

"TM takes only twenty minutes a day," a young widower told her. "I do it with my kids and it calms us all down."

As Daniel's mother drove home through the darkness, she decided to enroll.

"Guess what we're going to do?" she announced the next morning. Daniel and his sisters were at the kitchen table, eating frozen waffles they had revived in the toaster and saturated with Lite, imitation syrup. Everything they ate now came from boxes, from vacuum-packed foil envelopes and tiny, modular trays they popped into the microwave themselves.

"We're going to learn transcendental meditation," their mother said. She used the same tone, Daniel noticed, that she used whenever she wanted them to vacuum the living room or help wax the car. He squirmed in his chair and looked at his waffle, disintegrating in a puddle of syrup. Of the word "transcendental," only the "dental" part registered.

"Transcendental meditation? Oh God, Mother. Just what on earth is that?" said his sister, Lydia, lighting a cigarette. Lydia was fifteen. She wore her sunglasses around the house and a red kimono her boyfriend had given her for Christmas. Before their father left, Lydia wouldn't have dared smoke at the table.

"It's a relaxation process," their mother said, yanking the cigarette from Lydia's fingers and mashing it out in a saucer. Their mother smoked, too, but only in the bathroom. Daniel caught her once, perched like a sparrow on the lid of the toilet seat, blowing smoke nervously out the window in small, breathy puffs.

"Each person gets a mantra," she explained, "a secret word designed especially for them. You say it over and over, and it makes you feel peaceful." She looked pointedly at Lydia. "Given the mood in this household lately, I think we could use it."

Lydia snorted and pushed her sunglasses up the bridge of her nose.

Daphne put down her fork and chewed thoughtfully. Syrup framed her mouth in sticky parentheses.

"What if you forget your word?" she asked.

Daphne was seven, with an open pudding face. She was nothing more than chubby, really, though the kids in her class called her "chunky monkey." It did not help that she was also bookish and eager to please. Whenever kids teased her, she cried and bargained with them to stop—which only, of course, made them more vicious. Often, Daniel had to defend her. When kids pecked at her in the school yard, he pushed them aside, put an arm around his sister's trembling shoulders, and ordered, "Leave her alone." He was a fifth grader. Nobody challenged him.

"You don't forget a mantra," their mother assured her. "And if you do, you can always go back to the meditation center and have them tell it to you again."

"Sounds like horseshit to me," Lydia said.

Daniel gave her a look.

"What?" said Lydia. "Am I talking to you?"

Their mother got up and walked to the sink. She turned on the faucet and stood over it for a minute, her knuckles pressed against the counter. She was working ten hours a day now at Hudson's department store, standing behind the cosmetics counter in a boxy pink suit and high heels, spraying women's wrists with Obsession. At night she came home stinking of gardenias. She sat in the living room soaking her feet, eating ice milk out of the carton, watching reruns of "Cheers."

The weekend before, Lydia had sauntered in wearing a green taffeta dress. It had a sweetheart neckline and a short flared skirt. Daniel knew this dress belonged to their mother. There was photograph of her wearing it, framed in their hallway. It showed her at a Christmas party the year before she was married. She was sitting on their father's lap. His arm was hooked around her waist, and they were both holding highballs and laughing into the camera.

"I'm going out," Lydia had announced, the green fabric rustling against her legs. She had on a motorcycle jacket as well, and clunky black shoes and an oversized crucifix on a black cord around her neck. Daniel thought she must be kidding.

Their mother set down her spoon. "Why did you borrow that without asking?" she said.

"What do you care?" Lydia shrugged. "It's not like you have any dates."

Daniel had known that this was not the right thing to say. The foot basin sloshed, and their mother got up. She hobbled over to Lydia and slapped her clean across the mouth. For a minute, Lydia stood there gaping. Then her face turned bright red and she screamed, "No wonder Daddy left us."

Daphne began to cry.

"We all need to learn ways to calm ourselves down," their mother said now, returning to the table with a glass of water, which she set down like a gavel. "It's important for a family." She took a TM brochure from her pocket. It was folded, accordian-style. She smoothed it out on the table as if it were a treasure map, a road atlas: *this way to happiness.* On one panel was a picture of the Maharishi. His beard and his hair were dishwater gray; the beard hung to his navel. To Daniel, he looked like a walrus. He wondered why wise men were always old and peculiar looking.

"*A mantra is a very special tool,*" their mother read. "*Children should not regard it as a toy bought for them by their parents and easily discarded. Instead, they should regard it as a gift they have purchased themselves. . . .*"

"If I was going to buy myself a gift, it certainly wouldn't be a mantra," murmured Lydia.

Their mother lowered the booklet. "Who asked you?" she said.

"Fine," Lydia said. "If nobody asked me, then I don't have to go." She shoved her chair away from the table, stood up, and stalked out of the room. Their mother kept reading, but Daniel could see her back stiffen.

"Well," she said brightly, refolding the brochure.

Daniel tried to smile back. His mother looked pale. Nowadays, her eyes were swollen, and she often sat with her head cocked, as if listening for a sound in the distance.

"But what if we forget our word?" Daphne asked again. Sometimes, Daniel thought, Daphne was so stupid.

He looked down into the well of his milk glass. It used to be, he'd wake up before sunrise, pad into the kitchen, and eat Pop-Tarts by himself, straight from the box. His father would come down a little while later, dressed for work, and stand behind him, staring out the window. His father wouldn't say anything, but together they'd watch the sun come up, and Daniel could always feel him there, gripping the back of his chair.

Daniel wondered where his father was now. He imagined him in a hotel room in a small western town full of cactus and tumbleweeds. His beat-up suitcase lay unopened on a table; the television was on, full volume and ignored. Their father had not left abruptly. He had drifted away from the family a little piece at a time. He would sit in his armchair, staring vacantly at the fake fireplace he'd installed, drinking a beer. He was a postman, and for a while, their mother explained his despondency as simple fatigue. "All day long, he's dealing with people," she said.

One night, Daniel awoke to find his father sitting at the foot of the bed, his lips moving rapidly, though he was not speaking. He seemed terribly sad. "Dad," Daniel had said sleepily, "wanna hear a riddle?"

Another night, Daniel awoke to see his father standing over him, framing his face with his fingers, as if he were preparing to photograph it.

"Dad," Daniel whispered, "are you okay?"

His father started, then nodded vigorously. "You need lists," he said hoarsely. "But you shouldn't write them down."

In the mornings, they began getting phone calls after Daniel's father had left for the post office: *Hello, is Mr. Raft there? He hasn't shown up for work*. Mail was piling up, packages were sitting undelivered in the truck. And so the dress rehearsals started. First he was gone a day, then a week, then a month. By the time he left for good, it was difficult for Daniel to think of him as the same father he'd had just a few years before.

Sometimes, Daphne asked Daniel if he thought their father would ever come back, if he had left because she was bad.

"He left because he was sick," Daniel said. "He had something wrong with him so he couldn't be happy." This, at least, was what his mother had explained, what he tried to believe.

"Are you two with me?" their mother asked now, waving the brochure. "Next week, we'll learn transcendental meditation, huh? Begin a new chapter in the old book of life?"

Daphne scrunched up her face and spit out some waffle. "Eeww," she groaned. Daniel kicked her under the table.

"Sure, Mom," he said. "We're with you."

He got up from the table and put his dish in the sink. Through the window, he could see the clothes tree in their backyard, revolving gently in the wind. It looked like an umbrella stripped bare by a storm.

Daniel's mother could only take them to the Lotus Flower Holistic Arts Center on her lunch break, so they had to get excused from school early. When

Daniel handed his teacher the note, he looked down at his sneakers and hoped she wouldn't ask questions. The idea of anyone finding out about transcendental meditation mortified him. Most kids he knew went to the Y after school for swimming and basketball; their parents bought them video games and took them to Dairy Queen. None of them got yanked out of school to go see a maharishi. No one he knew had a mantra.

On the school bus that morning, he instructed Daphne, "Don't tell anybody where Mom is taking us today or they'll tease you even harder." Daphne nodded, sucked on a Life Saver, hugged her Simpsons lunch box, and stared out the window.

As it turned out, his teacher said only, "At a quarter to one, I'll give you a nod." She was a kind woman, who had heard about Daniel's situation at home and was genuinely concerned, though Daniel, of course, did not know this. Twice a week during recess, his teacher sent him to see Ingrid Beales, the school guidance counselor. Daniel sat at a low blond table drawing with Magic Markers, while Ingrid stood over him like a sentry, making observations: "You seem to be depressed today, Daniel. Would you like to discuss it?"

One wall in Ingrid's office was covered with elaborate certificates decorated with gold seals. The other had children's drawings on it—mostly scribble-scrabble full of monsters and teeth.

"Are you having trouble sharing?" Ingrid would ask.

"No," Daniel would answer. "I just don't have anything to say."

Occasionally, if he was in the mood, he might tell her a little about basketball, or about Fig, his pet newt, whom he kept in a jar on his windowsill. Once, after Daphne had gotten pushed off the monkey bars at recess, he did say he wished other kids would just mind their own business and leave her alone.

"You must feel a lot of responsibility," said Ingrid, nodding vigorously.

When Daniel got tired of drawing, he played with her magnetized paperweight, and piled alphabet blocks on top of one another, until the tower grew so high it tumbled down by itself. He never told Ingrid about his stomach—that there was a steady burning in it, as if someone had stabbed it with a lit cigarette and now a hole was growing there, a little wider each day.

It was raining when their mother came to pick them up, and Daniel and Daphne had to dash through the puddles.

"Did you tell your teacher why you were leaving early?" his mother asked as they climbed, dripping, into the car. She had come straight from Hudson's and was still in her work clothes, her "Cynthia" name tag pinned lopsidedly on her blouse.

"Nope," said Daniel, staring straight ahead at the dashboard.

"Daphne?" his mother said, eyeing her in the rearview mirror. "What about you?"

"Nuh-uh," Daphne said, yanking the seatbelt across her lap. "I didn't want the kids to call me a retard."

Their mother sighed. "TM is nothing to be ashamed of, you know," she said, twisting the key in the ignition. The car shuddered. "A lot of famous people meditate. Sting. Cher. The Beatles, before they broke up. Tina Turner—"

"Who's she?" asked Daphne.

"That comedian you kids like—what's his name—who screams at the audience."

"He's dead," Daniel mumbled. The windshield wipers squeaked back and forth, and he listened to them, hearing a jingle: *I'm awake, you're asleep. I'm a cake, you're a creep.*

"Mom," said Daphne, "afterward, can we go to Dairy Queen?"

The Lotus Flower Holistic Arts Center was located in the far corner of the Fishkill shopping mall, directly above a Wow, It's Yogurt! shop and next door to a travel agent. A pink neon squiggle hung in the window beside a simple, hand-lettered sign: LOTUS FLOWER HOLISTIC ARTS CENTER–ALL ARE WELCOME. As they entered, a little bell tinkled over the door. The air smelled of ointment.

"Hello?" their mother called.

Inside was a metal reception desk, an overstuffed sofa and thick wine-colored carpeting. It reminded Daniel of a doctor's office, except batik bed-spreads were tacked over the windows, giving the room a hermetic, wintry feel. Posters of the Maharishi were framed on the walls. Behind the reception desk was a small shelf arranged with votive candles and stalks of gladiola. A stick of incense was burning in a brass holder—its resiny smoke curdling the air. There were no tables, Daniel noticed, and no magazines.

"Hello?" his mother called again.

Daniel's stomach tightened. "No one's here, Mom," he said. "I think we should go."

"This place is weird," said Daphne.

Just then there was a rustling. A smiling woman in a stretchy white turtle-neck emerged from a sheet tacked over a doorway.

"Hello, hello, hello," she said breathlessly. "Can I help you?"

She was the skinniest woman Daniel had even seen; her ribs pressed through her pullover like the teeth of a comb. She spoke so softly, Daniel thought maybe the Maharishi was asleep in the back and she did not want to wake him.

"I'm Cynthia Raft," Daniel's mother said. Her voice, he noticed, had also dropped to a whisper. "My children and I have an appointment to learn TM."

"Ah, yes, yes, yes," the woman smiled. She opened a big leather appointment book and scanned a list of entries. "Cynthia, Daphne, Daniel and Lydia," she read.

"Well, Lydia's not coming," said Daniel's mother.

"Oh," the woman frowned. "I see." She seemed to take this personally.

"She's fifteen," said Daniel's mother. "It's a phase, I guess." She laughed nervously and drew her purse in front of her. "I hope."

"Well, to everything there is a season," the woman said. "I'm Lucy." Daniel noticed Lucy had a dark gap between her front teeth. Her long, oily hair was parted severely in the middle, as if someone had made an incision in her scalp. "Come," she motioned. "Have you brought your offerings?"

Daniel's mother rummaged through her purse and handed Lucy a fat white envelope. The initiation fee for transcendental meditation was two hundred dollars. Their mother had gotten a cash advance from Hudson's.

"Good," Lucy smiled. Then she turned to Daniel and Daphne. "And the children's?"

In order to show their "dedication to the Maharishi," the TM center required all children to donate a week's allowance to him. When their mother had told them this, Daphne threw a temper tantrum and Lydia snorted, "TM obviously stands for Take Money or for Total Morons." As punishment, their mother had donated Lydia's allowance as well, and this had led to another big fight.

"The children's money is in there with mine," their mother said.

"That's my whole allowance," said Daphne.

Lucy placed the envelope in a small brass box on the shelf beneath the poster and locked it. Then she turned around and smiled at them beatifically. "The Maharishi thanks you," she said.

She lead them back to a small, chilly room where they sat on folding chairs and watched a filmstrip. It showed a young man in a flower necklace sitting on a hill, speaking to the camera. His voice was slow and dreamy. Daniel wondered if he had just woken up from a nap.

"Transcendental meditation uses simple phonetic sounds to synchronize the natural rhythms of your mind and body with those of the universe," the man said.

Daniel had no idea what he was talking about. He glanced at his mother, sitting beside him. In the flickering light, her profile was lovely and unblinking, and he hoped she would notice him. When she didn't, he slumped in his seat and fumbled around in his pockets. He found an old throat lozenge and stuck it in his eye like a monocle. He hoped to see the world turn red, but the lozenge was coverd with lint. He sat up, scratched, and played with the scab on his elbow. He noticed Lucy, standing in the doorway, watching the screen intently. He wished he had brought Fig along. Though you weren't supposed to, you could put a newt in your pocket. "Transcendental meditation improves people's concentration," said the man in the film.

The end showed the Maharishi, who had yet to say a word, sitting cross-legged in the grass. He smiled and nodded stiffly, as if he had recently broken his neck. Then the lights came on and Lucy stood before them. "Okay, Daniel," she said. "Why don't you come with me first."

Daniel grimaced, but his mother patted him on the shoulder. "Go on," she whispered. "This will be good for you."

Lucy led him into a small room with two ornate armchairs facing a picture of the Maharishi. It was the same picture Daniel had seen in the brochure. Beneath it was another small shelf decorated with candles, carnations and the strong, musky incense that made Daniel queasy.

"Sit," Lucy instructed, motioning to one of the chairs. She turned off the overhead lights and sat down beside him.

"Daniel," she said. She took each of his hands in hers and stared into his eyes. Her tone was very somber; he could feel her breath on his face. She reminded him of Ingrid Beales. "I am going to give you your mantra. Do you know what that is?"

Daniel nodded.

"This is a very special word, Daniel. It is designed especially for you. It cannot be shared with anyone else, or it will no longer work. Do you understand?"

Daniel nodded again, though his stomach was in spasms. "Not even your little sister, or your mother, Daniel, can know this word."

Daniel wondered how the Maharishi and this woman knew him well enough to come up with a word suited exactly to his personality. He hoped it would be "basketball," or better yet, "newt." At least, he hoped, it would begin with a "D."

"Okay, Daniel," Lucy said, squeezing his hand. "Close your eyes."

Daniel closed his eyes.

"Now repeat after me," she said. "*Om.*"

Every evening after that, they were all supposed to meditate. When their mother didn't have to go to class, she set the kitchen timer and they did TM together in the living room, their eyes closed, the air silent and heavy between them. Since Daphne was so young, she was allowed to meditate by walking around in circles, following the edge of the rug. Daniel sat in his father's old chair facing the fireplace; his mother sat on the loveseat to his left. Always,

Daniel had the urge to peek to see if Daphne was cheating, but he worried his mother would check up on them and catch him in the process. Occasionally, he snuck looks at her, half expecting to see her watching him, but her eyes were always squeezed closed and there was a tremulous look on her face, as if she were praying.

The nights she went to school, she called from the employee lounge at the store. "Okay," she told Daniel, "you and Daphne go meditate for ten minutes. I'll do the same right here and call when I'm done."

Daniel sat on his bed and shut his eyes so tightly that orange and magenta cauliflowers formed beneath his lids. "Om," he hummed to himself, stretching the "Os" like a yawn.

He was supposed to say this over and over until it became as rhythmic and involuntary as breathing. But no sooner did he start Om-ing, than other thoughts crept into his head. He was suddenly aware of the sound of people raking leaves outside—the metallic scrape of it, the crunching underfoot—and of the staccato warble of the television next door, and of dogs barking, of windows shuddering in the October wind, of car tires crunching over gravel, pans clattering in the kitchen, Lydia's radio: *And now, on WKMY, your all-rock station, here's the latest from Pearl Jam.* . . . He could hear his own breathing, the delicate wheeze of it, his lungs collapsing and reinflating themselves in unison, his heart thumping gently behind his ear like fingertips on a table.

Advertising jingles glided lazily around his mind like biplanes. He thought of his Michael Jordan basketball card and a jump shot he himself had made in gym class. He thought of Audrey Plummer, the girl who sat in the desk in front of him, who peeked at his science quiz and wore sequined barrettes. He thought of his father's face, with its sad black mustache and inscrutable eyes. He thought about how his father used to rumple his hair and say, "Dan, my little man."

Each time Daniel's thoughts got away from him, he tried to rein them in. Om, he kept thinking. Om, om, om. If you did TM correctly, he imagined, it felt like flying, a breeze washing over your face.

Yet the more he sat there, the bedspread nubby beneath his palms, the more he could only remember overhearing his mother telling the story of how she and his father had met: his father, eighteen and crew-cutted, trudging up her front porch to deliver a package on a hot July afternoon, while she, barely sixteen, sat playing hearts on the porch with her girlfriends.

"Special delivery," his father had said. His mother had casually glanced up from her cards and realized he was staring at her. He became flustered and dropped a few letters. Then he tipped his postman's cap and apologized. It was ninety-three degrees out and his hair was shiny with perspiration. Her girlfriends began to giggle.

"He was so boyish and handsome," his mother recalled. "I invited him in for a Coke. He wasn't supposed to stop at all but he stayed ten minutes and asked me out as he left."

Daniel imagined his father now, roaming alone somewhere out West, nothing but parched land for hundreds of miles between them. The world was airless, a pre-tornado calm, the skies yellowing to soupy green, growing warm and moist with danger. The wind was blowing, and dust was enveloping his father, obscuring his face. Daniel's neck jerked then. He had started to nod off. By the time he began his mantra again, his stomach hurt.

After a while, whenever his mother called to remind them to meditate, he simply sat on his bed and played with Fig. He could hear Lydia downstairs, setting the table for dinner, banging each piece of silverware down on the table and grumbling, "Defrost already!" He could hear her punching the buttons on the microwave with small, digital bleats. It occurred to him to go and help her, but then, then she would know. "Forget your mantra?" she would say archly.

"How was your meditation?" his mother asked when she arrived home. Her eyes were beginning to look like they had been smudged with purple chalk.

"Great," Daniel said. Behind him, Daphne stood nodding.

"Great, too," she said.

Their mother smiled wearily. "Oh, I'm so happy to hear that," she said, looking not at them, but at Lydia, who was sitting in the living room watching television, refusing to look up. "I'm feeling so much more relaxed myself, I really can't begin to tell you," their mother added. Her voice sounded odd to Daniel, as if she were trying to sell something. Then she went into the kitchen and began filling a basin with Epsom salts, sighing loudly.

Six weeks later, the skies grew frigid and gray. Stores began displaying gift boxes and stenciling snowflakes onto their windows with white powder. Daniel's mother filled their somber house with colored lights and bought a wreath for the front door, where it hung like a life preserver. An invitation arrived from the Lotus Flower Holistic Arts Center for a "young meditators" Christmas party. *The Maharishi and his family of followers cordially invite you*, it began. Daniel's mother urged him and Daphne to go.

"It will be fun," she said. "You'll meet other children with mantras."

The center was decorated with white gauzy material that was supposed to be snow. In the middle of the screening room was a Christmas tree draped with garlands of popcorn. A buffet table was set up in the corner. Clumps of poinsettias lined the shelf beneath the Maharishi's picture.

"How lovely," their mother said as they entered, bundled like onions in their thick sweaters and coats. "I wish I could stay."

Daniel noticed the other children in the room. Most of them were younger than he, and a few had the sullen, vaguely cockeyed look of students in a special-ed class. As Lucy came over to greet them, one of the mothers handed her a prescription bottle.

"Jeffrey gets one of these at four, another at six," she instructed. "Otherwise he goes through the roof."

Her son, dressed in a green-and-white rugby shirt, was standing by the buffet table, picking cashews out of a tin of assorted nuts and stuffing them into his mouth. He was taller than the other kids and looked about twelve.

Daniel's mother kneeled down and kissed Daphne on the forehead. "I've got to get back to work," she said. Daniel looked at the floor and chewed on the inside of his cheek.

"Hey," his mother chided, "why the sad face? Cheer up, little man. You're at a Christmas party."

"Mom," he whispered, glancing worriedly at the other kids. "I don't know about this."

She looked at him for a second, then at Daphne, who had run over to the Christmas tree. "Well, do me a favor," she said softly, cocking her head in Daphne's direction. "Just give it a try, okay?"

Daniel looked down at the rug and nodded. His mother smiled and rumpled his hair. "Attaboy" she said. Then she handed a bag of oranges to Lucy as their offering to the Maharishi.

"I should be back by seven," she said.

The firt thing Lucy did was have them go around the room and introduce themselves. Most of the children mumbled; Daniel could not hear their names except for Jeffrey's and those of identical twins, Laura and Lara, who were dressed in matching red-and-green outfits. When it got to his turn, he said simply, "I'm Daniel Raft. I'm ten," and hoped no one noticed him.

"I'm his sister," added Daphne, forgetting to say her name.

When they finished, Lucy clapped her hands. "Okay everybody," she said. She was wearing the same white turtleneck and jeans she'd worn when Daniel first met her, except now she also had on a Santa Claus hat, its pom-pom dangling beside her cheek like a bellpull. "Before we have all our Christmas goodies, why don't we meditate?"

The kids groaned.

"We wanna eat," shouted Jeffrey.

"Now, now," said Lucy. "If we eat before we meditate, it'll slow our digestion."

"Food," Jeffrey chanted. "Food, food."

Some of the other kids picked up his cue and started chanting, "food, food, food," like a mantra.

Lucy laughed and shook her head. "First we meditate," she said. "Come on, stand up. We're going to have a group session."

Grudgingly, the children rose to their feet. Daniel saw Daphne eye the buffet table longingly. He wished he were anywhere else.

"We'll meditate in a circle, marching around the Christmas tree," Lucy said. "Everybody join hands."

Daniel reached for Daphne's left palm, grateful that he was not in this alone. Nobody else wanted to hold hands, however, and Lucy had to coax them.

"This is stupid," said Jeffrey, crossing his arms. "I'm not marching."

"Well then, Jeffrey," Lucy said, "you won't get any goodies later."

"If I go around in circles, I'll get dizzy and puke."

"Then sit in a chair," Lucy said.

Jeffrey sat down and grinned triumphantly at the others in a way that made Daniel uneasy.

"Now, everyone close their eyes and begin marching," Lucy instructed.

Daniel waited to make sure everyone else did it first, then followed. Instead of thinking of his mantra, he concentrated on not stumbling over the rug. He was aware of the creaking of the floor and the fact that he must look ridiculous. He peeked to see if anyone was watching.

"Lucy, Daniel's peeking," Jeffrey announced. "I just saw him."

A few kids started giggling.

"Everyone shush and say your mantras," said Lucy. "Jeffrey, you're supposed to have your eyes closed."

For a few more minutes, they circled the tree in silence. Daniel began to daydream that his father would reappear on their doorstep Christmas morning, though in his heart, he knew better. Three Christmas vacations ago, his father had taken him along with him on his morning rounds. Daniel had gotten to ride in the mail truck and carry some of the envelopes as they walked up the paths to the mailboxes. In the afternoon, they stopped for lunch—chili dogs and chocolate milkshakes—and afterward, back at the post office, Daniel's father let him play with the rubber stamps. Daniel wondered what his father would think if he saw them now in the meditation center. He glanced quickly at Daphne, but could not tell if she was enjoying this. His stomach felt like it had welts in it. Just then somebody burped and everyone giggled.

"Please, people," Lucy said. "We've got two more minutes. Concentrate."

But then the person farted and everyone, including Daniel and Daphne, started laughing.

"Hey, everybody," Jeffrey shouted. "Who wants to hear my mantra?"

"Now, none of that," said Lucy. She was still smiling her wiry, puppet's smile, but Daniel could tell she was getting annoyed. "Behave yourselves and you can eat now."

Within seconds, everyone broke out of the circle and crowded around the buffet, pushing and grabbing. Daniel could barely get near it. When he did, he saw that Lucy had made elaborate designs with all of the snacks. Dried apricots were arranged like flower petals, dates were decorated with peanut halves to look like tiny racing cars. But the treats were all healthy—organic fruit juice bars, raisins, carrot sticks.

"Don't you have any real food?" the twins whined.

"What the hell is this stuff?" said Jeffrey. "Fungus?"

Somebody stomped her feet. Daphne whispered, "I wanted brownies."

Eventually, everyone ate what they could, leaving the floor strewn with paper plates and half-eaten fruit bars. Lucy tried to engage them in various clapping games afterward, but no one was interested. Daniel wished he had stayed home with his newt.

"All right," Lucy said finally, her voice growing brittle. "I was going to save this for last, but we'll do it now."

She led them all to the room where Daniel had first learned his mantra. Suspended from the ceiling was a strange lavender globe covered with petals of pink and purple crepe paper. Long, stiff green spears jutted out from its base. It was the size of a beach ball, and as it twirled lazily from its rope, Daniel could see bits of newsprint through the cracks in the paper.

"Does anyone know what this is?" Lucy asked.

There was silence.

"It's a lotus flower," Daphne said, softly from the back.

The rest of the kids turned and looked at her. Daniel was impressed. It was a lotus flower, he could see now, a giant one, made of papier-mâché.

"That's right," said Lucy. "Do you know what else?"

The kids shook their heads. It was a piñata, Lucy said: a gift from their TM center in Mexico. She explained how it was stuffed full of prizes, and asked the children if they wanted to open it.

"Yeah!" everyone chorused.

Lucy went over to the corner and got a broomstick and a handkerchief.

"Daphne," she said. "Since you knew what this was, would you like to try first?"

Daphne looked questioningly at Daniel. "Say yes," he whispered. Daphne still hadn't grasped that being first was an honor.

"Okay," Daphne said. She reached for the broomstick.

"Wait," Lucy said. "First, we've got to blindfold you."

She shook the handkerchief out across Daphne's face, and fleetingly Daniel could see his sister's eyes behind it, widening with worry. Once Daphne was blindfolded, Lucy placed the broomstick tightly in her hands.

"Okay, everyone. Give us some room," Lucy instructed.

As the children formed a ring around her, she gripped Daphne by the shoulders and spun her, chanting, "Around and around she goes."

When Lucy finally released her, Daphne was reeling. She stumbled blindly around the rug, flailing at the air with the broomstick. The piñata hung behind her, a large purple sun. Daniel suddenly realized that this might not have been the best idea. He got down on his haunches and whispered, "Daphne, turn around."

Daphne spun around in a circle, swiping at nothing.

"Go right, go right!" the kids screamed. Daphne tripped forward and the broomstick smacked against the wall.

"Wrong way, Daff," Daniel coached.

"Go left!" the children yelled.

Daphne headed in the other direction, and this time when she swung, the broomstick made a gash in the side of the lotus and bits of candy and paper came trickling out.

The kids cheered. "That's it, Daff. Again," Daniel said.

Daphne swung the stick like a baseball bat. In her eagerness, she lost her balance and fell backward, missing the piñata entirely and landing on her backside. The kids started laughing. "Get up and hit it!" Jeffrey shouted.

Daphne struggled to get up, but dropped the broomstick. She began feeling around the rug on her hands and knees. Daniel glanced worriedly around the room. He spied Lucy leaning against the wall, massaging her temples, her hair lank curtains on either side of her face.

"Daff, it's by your feet," Daniel said.

"The stick's right by your feet, you moron!" Jeffrey shouted.

This seemed to revive Lucy. "Jeffrey, we'll have none of that," she called over.

"Pick it up!" the kids yelled. "Pick it up and hit it!"

Daphne continued to grope. She was wearing woolen tights, and the static created by her knees against the rug was making her dress ride up. The backs of her legs and her behind became exposed, and the white of her underwear was visible through the weave of her tights. "Hee hee, look at her underpants," someone said. "What a fat butt!"

The children began laughing. Daphne grew flustered. Daniel's heart pounded. He searched for Lucy, but the children began packing around him, trying to get a better look at Daphne.

"Fat butt," they chanted again. Shakily, Daphne managed to find the broomstick. She staggered up, hacking at the air.

"Hit it!" kids shouted. Daphne struck the flower again, but only lightly enough to send it swinging back and forth over her head like a pendulum.

"Jesus Christ, blimp-o, can't you do anything?" Jeffrey shouted. Daphne's dress was still sticking up in the back.

"Fat butt," the children hooted. "Fat butt. Fat butt. I see London! I see France—"

"People, that's enough," Lucy said.

"I see Daphne's underpants!"

"Leave her alone!" Daniel said as they hooted and squirmed around him.

"Fat butt, fat butt!"

Daniel could see tears starting to slide down Daphne's face from underneath the blindfold. "Ignore them, Daff," he called.

"People, if you don't stop, we'll end the party right now," Lucy shouted.

Daphne's arms dropped to her side then and she began to cry. Daniel dashed over and picked up the broomstick. Raising it high over his left shoulder, he gave a shrill whoop and brought it down hard on the piñata, smashing it in half. Chocolate coins, kazoos, pieces of bubblegum splattered everywhere; the lotus swung back and forth crazily, gushing candy.

"Daniel!" said Lucy.

Daniel whooped again and began bashing away at the remains of the piñata, its papery skull deflating with each blow.

"Daniel, stop it!"

Daniel threw down the broomstick and lunged at Jeffrey. The two of them fell to the floor, tumbling over each other, clawing and kicking. A chair got knocked over. Daniel straddled Jeffrey and got in two good punches before being thrown to the rug. Jeffrey rolled on top of him, but Daniel got his hands locked around Jeffrey's throat. Around them, kids were cheering, others scrambling on their hands and knees, grabbing as much candy as possible.

"Daniel, Jeffrey, please!" Lucy cried. "Everybody stop! Stop! Center yourselves!"

Behind her, the Maharishi's picture smiled vacantly over their heads.

The wind was strong, and overhead, scalloped Christmas decorations swung from the lampposts like bells. Their mother arrived with Lydia, who hurried with her across the parking lot. Daniel saw them through the plate glass window of the Wow, It's Yogurt! shop, where he sat with Daphne and the twins eating sundaes, their faces a riot of chocolate and syrup. The other kids' parents had all come and gone, leading their children away by the wrist.

Daniel's nose and front teeth still hurt. Blood was caked around his left nostril. The frozen yogurt, however, was a salve on his tongue, cooling his throat and the grill of his stomach.

Lucy leaned beside the glass door, the Santa Claus hat wilted in her hand. As Daniel's mother and sister approached, she swung the door open.

"They're in there," she muttered, without looking up.

Their mother and Lydia headed for the table. Their mother was still in her work clothes, and Lydia was wearing an oversize coat that belonged to her boyfriend.

"So, I hear you two really achieved inner peace." Lydia grinned.

"Mom," Daphne said apologetically, setting down her spoon. "Daniel was just defending me."

"I don't want to hear it," their mother said, snatching up their scarves. "Get your coats on and let's go." Then she saw Daniel's nose, his swollen upper lip. "Oh, Jesus," she sighed. She dropped down beside him and touched her palm to his cheek. "Are you all right?"

Daniel swallowed and nodded. "Uh-huh," he said. "Just a bloody nose."

Lydia put a hand over her mouth and glanced away. Daniel could tell she was stifling a laugh. When she turned back around, she flashed him a thumbs-up sign and whispered, "Yeah! Nailed 'em!" Their mother paid Lucy for the yogurt and ushered them out of the store.

On the ride home, nobody said much. Their mother took a pack of cigarettes out of her purse, removed one with her teeth, then tossed it to Lydia. They both sat there, exhaling their fumes out of opposite windows, threads of smoke weaving between them.

In the back, Daphne took out the plastic kazoo she had gotten from the piñata and blew a few notes of "I'm a Yankee Doodle Dandy." Daniel expected their mother to turn around and tell her to be quiet, but she didn't. He sat calmly, listening to Daphne play, his cheek pressed against the cool of the window. Shadows and lights from the highway washed over his face, and beyond the glass, he could see the dark trees passing by, the small, shingled houses glittering with Christmas lights, their doors flanked by candles, tiny crèches huddled on their lawns, evergreens winking with strings upon strings of fake stars, garish sleds led by reindeer leaping from rooftops into the thick bruise of the sky—everyone waiting in the darkness, for someone to arrive.

The Way Sin Is Said in Wonderland

1.

The first time they met, Eddie had pulled out a pistol. A Soviet Makarov nine-millimeter automatic with the rust spots and that faded red star on the black plastic handgrip. This was '72, the summer before the pullout, the occasion a welcome-home barbeque for Bobby, her husband, and his buddy from MR II up near Con Tien.

"This is I-Beam," Bobby said. "Short for IBM, he's smart."

Turned out he almost had a degree in physics from Rice University, but Carol Ann didn't know that yet; she only knew that he was a wiry so-and-so, slope-shouldered and skinny as a file but surprisingly soft-spoken, as if all Uncle Sam had asked him to do during his hitch was sit atop a jungle roost drinking skim milk and nodding hunky-dory to the dignitaries making merry on the promenade below.

"A pleasure," he said, and then nothing: just the two of them, the afternoon August sun pouring in over his head, while Bobby hurried away to say howdy to the new people coming through the gate into the backyard. "Eddie," he said, "L-for-Lonnie Heber."

She got her name out then, Carol Ann Mobley Spears, surprised by the mouthful it was, and what she did, second grade teacher at Zia Elementary near Pecan Acres south of town, and then she realized that her hand was still locked in his—a cold thing big as a paddle—and it crossed her mind when she again engaged his flat eyes that here was a fellow with secrets you might need a whole lot more than *open sesame* to find out.

Throughout the afternoon, she watched him. He took a chair near Bobby and didn't say much. Let Bobby do the bullshitting. "Should I tell 'em about the S-2?" Bobby said once, and Carol Ann discovered Eddie Heber staring at her, grinning this time as if the two of them—he and she—had made a connection the shitkickers between them wouldn't comprehend if you wrote it down and drew pictures of the 3-D sort her second graders whooped over.

"Sure, whatever," Eddie said, and Bobby was off, his a story that seemed to take as long to tell as it did to live through.

She picked up a little—the LT, the boonie rats, the LURPs, Sam the Sham—before she went back to her conversation with Rhonda Whitaker and Ellen Dowling.

Rhonda's boy, Jerry, was deficient in history, plus being a cutup in class. Then she could feel him again, Eddie Heber. A smile with too much tooth in it. A face so alive it required concentration to watch. Spooky. He looked like a fugitive who had raced all night through prickers and brambles to get here.

That's the way it went until dusk. A volleyball game started, girls against guys, and every time she jumped or chased the ball when it rolled over to the Hoovers' fence, he was watching, this funny little fucker from Albuquerque. She felt naked, like a specimen, like the hamsters in the cage in the science corner of her classroom—just a piece of human business for his amusement. So after the third time she had to bend over in front of him, her shorts squeezing up her thighs, she thought she'd just march right up to him, get in his face, tell him she didn't appreciate his—what?—his leering, and he could just smack his lips somewhere else, she didn't care what had happened in Vietnam. But when she spun around, he was gone. His chair had a half-dozen empties beside it.

"C'mon," Bobby was saying, wanting the ball. "Let's go, Carol Ann. Everybody's waiting."

Then she saw him talking to Ellen Dowling by the keg, and he seemed bigger, more muscular, less bent and crabbed, a whole other human being—like something born in midair and half an idea that wouldn't make sense until you were eighty or eight thousand.

The Millers, Hank and that dimwit of his, Carla, went home first. About nine. After that, folks started drifting out in twos and threes—the Krafts, Mr. Preston, who owned the hardware store where Bobby, having flunked out of State, had worked after his reclassification to 1-A. "Welcome home, short stuff," they said. "Glad you're back." Then the Fosters took Rhonda home—she'd squabbled with George, her creepy husband, and he'd left with a couple of Bobby's old Bulldog teammates from Las Cruces High. About eleven, Margie and Louis Delgado said adios. Carol Ann was tired. Bobby had been home two days, and all he wanted to do was screw. Wanted her to take it from behind, wanted to do it with the lights on, like a ballfield. And all he'd talked about was this Eddie Heber. This primo buddy of his. Coming down from the Duke City for the cookout. "Me and Eddie," Bobby had said, "we were tight." *Tight*—a word Bobby'd wound up his whole face to say.

She'd taken three personal days, gotten the sub herself—Mrs. Feldman—done the lesson plans, made the slaw and the potato salad, called all the people, and now, watching Bobby scuttle back and forth like a dog between bones, she was beat, hollow as an echo. It wouldn't make any difference to Bobby: he'd want her anyway. He was feeling good—loosey-goosey, he called it. Wouldn't be spit to him that his buddy, Eddie L-for-Lonnie Heber, would be on the couch in the living room. You could hear through the walls in this place—that's what the builder was famous for, ticky-tack and walls you could poke your pinky through—but Bobby wouldn't care. He'd want to party. To shake his tail feathers. His phrase. Then, sudden as thunder, her thoughts flying every whichaway, Eddie was beside her, light-footed enough to be a ghost, his lips almost against her ear, his whisper a knot she couldn't find the beginning to.

"What?" she asked. Outside, Bobby was bear-hugging Sammy Vaughn and then playing grab-ass with Sammy's ex-wife Alice. Somewhere a car door slammed, and somebody—Harry Hartger?—was singing a Joe Cocker tune he didn't have the recklessness for, and here came Eddie Heber again—at the other ear this time—smelling of beer and charcoal and Jade East, his the voice the devil might have if it showed up in your living room near midnight to help you tidy up. "What?" she said.

"I said you're probably a heartbreaker, right?"

The pistol came out then. He reached under his shirt, a Hawaiian eyesore he later said he'd bought as a joke.

"I know you," he said, half his face closed, the other half open like a closet door. "I know your hair, the size of your shoe."

For a moment, Carol Ann thought it was a squirt gun or maybe a cap pistol—a toy as remarkable and cunning as ideas about life on Mars—and then, clearly, it wasn't, and when he pulled back the slide and it seemed entirely possible that a round had been chambered, she could see that he'd turned inside out again.

"You were a Zeta girl," he said. "Pledge chairman."

His jaw was slowly working, a sheen of sweat at his temples, his eyes beer-glazed and starting to go red at the corners, his breathing short and hard as if he were thinking about sex or had done the impossible—like carry the ocean to her in his arms all the way from California without spilling a drop.

"Over there," he was saying, "I saw your picture a million times. Made Bobby get me a copy."

Later—after she and Bobby divorced, after Eddie reentered her life—she remembered this moment for what didn't happen. She did not panic. She remembered turning toward him, not increasing by much the arm's length between them, just swiveling as if on a pivot. A man, marvelous as a maniac from a movie, was standing next to her. He seemed shiny and slick, more a figure sprung from her head than from another crossroads on earth. He had something in his hand—a gift, possibly—but her own hand was coming up to decline it. She remembered being clear-minded, her thoughts as shaped and ordered as pearls on a string, and after she gently pushed the gun aside she advanced on him, feeling his heat as she got closer, stopping at the point where, if her breasts brushed his shirt front, he might vanish like a soap bubble.

"I made up stories," he was saying. "You were wearing a dress, a white one. The boys at LZ Thelma loved that story."

Outside, Bobby was still goofing around. In a few minutes, he would want her, sloppy and rough and over in a wink. After that, she would sleep, scrunched over to the edge of the bed, the ex-PFC sprawled beside her about as easy to rouse as a log. It would be morning after that, and him starved for her anew.

"Where'd you get the gun?" she asked.

Firebase Maggie, he said. Belonged to a dink.

She was almost his height and close enough now to see he had excellent teeth, white as Chiclets. It seemed a tunnel had opened onto a distant and severe light.

"You kill him?" she wondered.

"Found it," he said. "A dozer dug it up when some concertina wire was being strung at the perimeter."

She was nowhere now, she thought. She had stepped through a gap—a seam, a tear—and whooshed into a world as deformed as dreamland itself. She had slipped through in an instant, quick as a wish, but she was not alone.

"You trying to scare me?" she asked. "Is that it?"

He seemed to ruminate then, something in his face gone to tilt, and it occured to her that he might be suffering from a fever. What was it they could get over there? Dengue or beriberi or malaria.

"I'm drunk," he said, but unslurred in a manner that gave her to understand he was sober as a surgeon.

"You sneaked up on me," she said. "That's not very sporting, Mr. Heber."

The other half of his face had come open now, as if a strong wind were blowing from his insides out.

"You get in the habit," he said. "It's like smoking."

It was then that she kissed him, tenderly at first and with her eyes open, him staring at her, too, but little in his expression to say he hadn't expected their love affair to commence this way, not even when, before she let go, she bit his lip. Hard.

"I bet you're a son-of-a-bitch, too," she said.

In 1986 they met again. It would turn out that he had been married as well, had three kids, all boys, who lived in Redondo Beach with their mother. He had been sliding, he would say. Drifting, coming undone—pick a word. Worked in aerospace for a while. LTV in Dallas. A computer company in San Antonio. Then—boom—a layoff. Squabbles. Fights. Tears like a river. Two days in jail in Houston. Worked the off-shore rigs for a time. Next a breakdown. Total. Bugs on the walls, the night sweats. Visions. Voices from the TV. It was the booze. It was want and venery.

She hadn't heard him come in. At her desk, school over for an hour, she was marking a spelling test. A-l-l-i-g-a-t-o-r. R-e-p-t-i-l-e. The cold-blooded family you were wise to step over on the great chain of being. She was thinking about her boyfriend after Bobby Spears, a rancher up the valley who raised polled Herefords. He liked to race motocross in the hills near Picacho Peak. Did impressions—Nixon, Porky Pig, Johnny Carson. Then, as if he'd materialized with a poof from a flash pot and a swell of horns from Hollywood, Eddie Heber was in the back of her room, sitting at Tiffany Garcia's desk, a cigarette going, his eyes flat again and abstract as math, and part of her seemed to have gone from wet to dry without any heat in between.

"If you're looking—" she began, but he shook his head. He'd found what he was looking for.

When he said her name, something caught in her chest—a bone, a hook of tissue—and the air sucked out of the room. She would have known him anywhere: a light, weird and cold as a glacier, seemed to come off his skin. He was too pale, too much of everything small and still and sad. His hair was long now, past his shoulders, as sleek and beautiful as a storybook Apache, longer than her own; and except for that, he seemed not to have been gone long at all, only minutes, as if he'd just stepped out to use the toilet; but when he rose, she could see that maybe his face had come off and had been put back in pieces, the features loose on his skull, parts from different puzzles of the same scene.

"You can't smoke in here," she said. "Mr. Probert has a cow if anyone smokes in the building."

She was apologizing, she realized, and suddenly felt too big for her clothes, her life too small for anything unrelated to Eddie Heber.

"You want to go for a ride?" he asked.

But when he sat near her, another desk scooted up tight, she understood they wouldn't be leaving for a few minutes yet. He seemed to be composing himself, pulling himself into a shape she wouldn't be frightened by. She was stunned by his size. He was bigger now—weights, she would learn; he'd done sixteen months in Parchman, in Arkansas, a fourth-degree assault—and she thought about him without his shirt, without any clothes whatsoever, between them only light and air and time.

He'd gone off the deep end, he said. It wasn't a Vietnam issue. It was human. The wires too tight. The gears spinning too hard. The twentieth century—all loop-de-loop and greed and the low road of scoundrels. Now he had a lawn and yard service. Greensweep. Been in town for over a year. Rented a house on Espina, up near the Armory.

He had shoved the words in her head. That's what she thought later, that he had not spoken at all—not using the old-fashioned organs of speech, at least—and that somehow it had become time for her own short story.

"Bobby Spears," she began.

He nodded, gravely. "A girlfriend. Betrayal."

Carol Ann caught herself looking at his cigarette, its smoke like a cloud with curls and a beard. Eddie Heber knew. Everything.

He and Bobby had had drinks about ten months ago, he said. At the El Patio bar in old Mesilla. Bobby Spears was a rock. He never changed.

"That was a long time ago," she said. "I'm better now."

In the silence, she could hear him breathing again, like that night over a decade before. His breath was language itself, she thought. It told you *who* and *why*, gave you information about the way you could behave, what you could expect. It wasn't complicated, just queer as reflections in a fun house.

"Where's the gun?" she asked. She had to get that settled.

He stubbed out his smoke on the bottom of his boot. His hands were coarse, the fingers long enough to play piano, the nails oddly well-manicured. Plus, he had a tatoo now, a dragon on his forearm—"jailhouse art," he would say eventually.

"Threw it away," he told her. Stepped out on the chopper platform—this was at Texaco 31—and pitched the weapon into the Gulf of Mexico.

She had stood, the flutter of her heart the only thing about this encounter that didn't surprise her.

"I want that ride now," she said.

Before they went to his place, he drove south on I-10, almost down to Anthony, then turned back north on old 85, the two-lane nearer the mostly muddy Rio Grande. Time seemed to have stopped, to be backing up on her, the air thick with heat, sunlight scattered everywhere in splinters and spikes.

He'd been crazed, he said. An affliction. Once he hadn't been able to use his hands. They'd been hooves. Mallets. Whole days had passed when he couldn't talk. He'd seen a doctor. Another. He was angry, he told them. Genuinely and profoundly pissed off. The world had failed him. He tried vitamins, yelling in the woods—the works. The world got runny at the edges. Cynthia vamoosed. She hadn't needed a lawyer because he'd given her everything—the Ford, the house, even the Oreos in his lunch bucket.

It was late now, the sky west of her, toward Deming, rich with blood and streaky clouds with orange undersides, everything too high and too filmy, and she thought she'd just awoken from a hard, terrible sleep—a sleep with too many people in it, too much jibber-jabber and too much peril to be alone in—and the first person who'd appeared to her upon waking was this man next to her, the one saying he hadn't made love to a woman in three years, maybe a little more. The pinching under her heart had started again, but Carol Ann found she had a place in her head where she could arrange herself against him.

In his driveway, he hurried around to her door and held out his hand—a gentleman. Touching him was like touching a circuit only God could flick the switch for—God, or another mystery said to be lavish with lightning and brimstone. And while he guided her up the sidewalk, she wondered how she would explain the peculiar turn of events to her colleagues, particularly Ruthie Evans, her best friend; or to her students when Eddie began picking her up in the parking lot; or even to Bobby Spears himself should she bump into him in the Food Mart. She was Carol Ann Mobley, she told herself. Her mother was Rilla, to honor an ancient relative in Texas; her daddy, Bill but called "Cuddy" by the cowboys who worked the ranch. She had other thoughts, but they proved impossible to collect. A wind, vicious as an argument, had come up to spread them willy-nilly. She believed she had asked him a question—"That night, what were you talking to Ellen Dowling about?"—and she believed he had answered—"You," he was thought to have said, "you and me"—but he was fumbling with his keys and all she could do was wait for the ground to cease shaking.

She seemed to recognize his house, the marvelous clutter inside. Afterward, she felt she'd suffered a vision, the present undone year by year until she was a child, a girl who was yet to grow up and go to college and meet a boy named Bobby, who would bring into her life a man named Eddie, who would unlock a door to the future she could barely walk through.

She was counting now—one-Mississippi, two-Mississippi—putting between herself and whatever was coming next the numbers she might one day get to the end of. Eddie Heber had sat her down, swept several magazines off the sofa—*People, The Statesman*, a much-thumbed Webster's paperback—and he put a club soda in her hand; he was talking to her, one word—love—coming at her again and again, his voice the last ton of a twenty-ton day. It was a replay, she believed. She had already done it: she'd already peeled off her clothes and urged him down on top of her. She'd already felt him, fretful and needy and clumsy but cool as wax, move her this way and that, her hips rising, her fingers on him there and there and there, the strangled noise he made trying to hold himself back, her hands not strong enough for his head, her legs hooked behind his knees, the carpet scratching her back, boxes and crates and motor parts the only items to look at except a face empty as a hoop.

Then it was over, the replay, and she was still dressed, out of numbers to count and soda to drink, and she had asked him if he was going to be bad for her. "Are you a bad man, Eddie?"

He hoped not, he said. But one never knew.

"One?"

A turn of phrase, he said. One as in you.

She was studying his living room, a corner of the kitchen, the hall. Back there was the bedroom, she guessed. One would have to rise, one would have to walk. A path led through the books, the unstable-looking piles of them, the titles as much about rocks and trees as they were about stuff you had to know to survive what daylight brought. Somehow, one would have to put oneself on that path, past the laundry in a heap, past the speaker cabinets and the snapshots that had spilled out of a sack.

Robert Ellis Spears, she thought. That was a man she had known, as were Karen Needham's brother and Tim Whitmire. J.T. Something-something, a mechanic with a scar across his nose. Another who'd imagined himself Conway Twitty, as dull a date as water was wet. A decision had been reached, she realized. Later, these were the rooms she remembered when she wondered where she had abandoned herself.

There: by the cushions. There: by the wobbly-looking table in a corner. There: near the end of a path to another door to pass through.

Now she was moving, her joints loose and oily, and Eddie had fallen in behind her, saying please excuse the mess. He was sorry. He'd intended to do more.

"That's all right," Carol Ann had told him.

She had given pieces of herself away—a piece to every man she'd ever loved—and now they were all coming back.

2.

He took her dreams first, little by little, the weight of them and their hue. She dreamed of her daddy's ranch outside Clovis, the land bleached and hostile and dry, and he took that. Eddie Heber. In junior high she had been a cheerleader, the Falcons, green and white pleated skirts with an applique megaphone stitched on the sweater. He took that, asking her to cheer for him, and applauded vigorously when she returned to bed. She'd broken her arm—her left—in a fall from a borrowed bike in front of her church. He grabbed that, and St. Andrew's itself, as well as the summer camp she went to in the moutains near Ruidoso. Her first snowman, her crush on Davy Crockett, "The Ed Sullivan Show," when she listened to the Beatles ask to hold her hand—he took those, and many times that first week she awakened with a start, her ears ringing, the sweat cold on her forehead, the sheets a tangle around her legs, and feared to see everything he'd taken suspended near the ceiling like stars to be oooohhhed over.

Other times she found him staring at her. Or a part of her. Her ankle. A mole on her shoulder. A shaving nick on her knee. It was like being watched by a plant. Once she found him with a penlight, bent to her chest in wicked concentration. "Don't move," he said. Nothing else in the room was visible, as if beyond the light was only blackness as void as space. The sheet around his shoulders, he smelled like well-water and Marlboros, rusty and bitter. "Ssshhh," he said. He had her lipstick, she noticed, a red so blue in this light it looked like ink. "You're beautiful," he said, the word as much made from iron and silver as from air and tongue and teeth.

He drew on her then, around her nipple, his mouth set hard as a knob, as if this were work that required precision and monklike patience, a version of top-secret science practiced underground. A moment later, he kissed her there, his lips soft as hair. A jolt surged through her, static going up her spine. She wanted to say *no* as much as she wanted to say *yes*. She was in her skin. And out. Close and far. He would ruin her, she thought. He would take her apart hook by hasp by hinge and put her back together topsy-turvy and jury-rigged, the outside in, the private as public as her face. Morning was coming, hazy and already squawky with birds in the tree outside their window, and she knew she'd soon find him on his back, his lips smeared and swollen and pink.

For days—when she wasn't at school and when he wasn't mowing lawns or hauling yard trash—they talked. It developed that he could cook. "Baked fruit curry," he would say, showing her with a flourish the cherries and the pineapples and the peach halves. "Dilly bread," he would say. "Eggplant casserole." They were announcements, these dishes. Declarations as formal as those that bigwigs got when they entered a ballroom to fanfare. In return, she told him about her wedding to Bobby Spears, the justice of the peace who'd performed the ceremony in the living room of her daddy's house, Bobby's haircut a whitewall like that he would get from Uncle Sam a year later. Her sorority sister Deedee Harrison had played the piano, "Cherish" by the Association. Her dress had come from Juarez, her own design of lace and satin and pearl buttons up the back. She had a lot to say, she felt, and Eddie was exactly the right person to hear the whole of it. He drank—Bacardi, George Dickel, Buckhorn beer—and she talked. He cooked—chocolate cream roll, tamale ring—and she told about her cousins, Julie and Becky Sims, and how her mother danced the Hully Gully and the first time she saw her father without his dentures, until the string of her had unwound and gone slack and she understood, less with her mind than with the worn muscle of her heart, that Eddie Heber was crazy.

"My boys," he said one evening. Eric and Willie and Eddie, Junior. They were like him—agile as waterbugs but scrawny, in and out of everything. They could cook, too. He'd learned it in the service—that's what he'd been, a chef, his MOS. An E-4 with a soupspoon. Cooked for the brass in Hotel Company with the 1/26. Petit four, salmon mousse, lemon meringue pie—as at home in a pantry as was Picasso in a garret in gay Paree. Working for Uncle Sugar was like working at the Hilton Inn. The mucky-mucks billeted in Airstream trailers, played golf on a three-hole course the Seabees had hacked out of the bush.

"Could've been Mexico," he said. "Puerta goddamn Vallarta."

Still in his work shirt, the sleeves rolled to the elbow, he was making almond macaroons. She'd spent the afternoon after school searching for rose water, three teaspoons of it, and now he was putting it together—the egg whites, the super fine sugar, the flour, the blanched nuts—moving between the baking sheet and his bottle of Black Jack on the counter. He'd become handsome, she thought. His hair was still long, tied back in a ponytail, his face now brown as a Mexican's, and she remembered that night, years and years before, when he was skinnier, drawn and wasted like a castaway, a man with a pistol and the hooded, melancholy eyes of a C-minus student. He had not been trying to scare her, she thought. Not really. He had been in love even then. Love could make you do anything, maybe howl or drive in a circle. Love might even involve guns.

Vietnam, he was saying. Best time of his life. Fucking aces high. Like "Bandstand" without the dress code. All the brutal business in the highlands or the Delta never got anywhere near him. Steppenwolf on the eight-track, Budweiser in the fridge. Direct phone link with the world. Tried to ring up Bob Dylan one night, tell the guy he was full of it. No answers were blowing in the wind. Hell, nothing blew over there. By comparison, R&R was a major disappointment. Couldn't wait to get back in-country and rustle up some Knickerbocker fritters for Xmas.

"That's not what Bobby said," she told him.

"Bobby," he said. He could've been referring to a tree he'd trimmed. "Bobby was a clerk. During the day, he typed COM/SIT reports, hustled the commissary files."

For a minute, she refused to believe it, a Polaroid of Bobby in camouflage coming to mind.

"He bought the outfit in Hong Kong," Eddie told her. "On Nathan Street. I got a suit, looked like one of the Temptations."

In the next hour — humbug pie, with raisins and molasses — he showed her more of himself. He'd been a liar, too, he confessed. In high school. At Rice. Sophomore year, for example, he'd told a girlfriend that his parents were dead. Marge and Gene. In a car wreck near Portales. They were alive, he said. Retired. They liked to ski — Sandia, Angel Fire over near Taos, up in Utah. His dad had worked for the air force, an engineer. His mom —

A question was coming, she realized. When he was finished, however long the current confession took, however roundabout the getting there, he would ask her something — about them, certainly, but also about the trees and the land and the humans who were upon it — and she would have to get an answer out without stuttering like an idiot who only lately learned English.

"Fix me a drink?" she asked.

He made her a Cuba Libre — too sweet, she would recall — and he told her about Cynthia.

Maiden name Lanier, he said. From Houston, a bona fide heiress. Oil. A million cousins and uncles, mostly in Louisiana. A gruesome people. All named Tippy or Foot or Beebum.

"You hit her," she said.

Once, he said. During a spell. Afterward, she'd sicced a mob of close relations on him. Spent a week in Baylor Medical.

The sun had gone down a while ago, and the kitchen, except for the fierce light over the stove, had become gloomy and choked with cigarette smoke. He was almost to the end of himself, she decided. All the bounce had left his voice, the ends of his sentences coming in whispers. Only dribs and drabs were reaching her: Fort Smith, Arkansas. A Starvin' Marvin. Behind the register, a female redneck, your basic sullen type. Light that turned the skin yellow as mustard. The walls wobbling. A quarrel about change. About the magazine rack. About the swirl the universe made going down the drain at his feet. Glass shattering, Pepsi bottles rolling like bowling pins. An arm, his own, sweeping along the service counter. *The Globe.* Castro playing voodoo with Kennedy's brain. Finally, a fist, his own. No more redneck standing up.

Just, when the cops arrived, Edward L-for-Lonnie Heber sitting splay legged in an aisle gobbling brown sugar from the bag.

"Eddie," she said.

She had his attention now, like being looked at by every peasant in China.

"Don't be crazy anymore, okay?"

"It's my temperament," he said. "I take offense."

He had put food in front of her—a wedge of pie and a macaroon, both cool now—and she tried to eat a little. The light was in her eyes, still harsh as a screech, so she made him turn it off. She was thinking about her job—the numbers and shapes and science she was employed to pass on to the children the neighborhood sent her. They liked geography, these kids. Tanika had chosen Zanzibar; Ellen Foley, Egypt. Cotton came from one place, copper from another. Everyone had a country to be responsible for—the tribes that rampaged the hinterlands, the chiefs who rose up to lead them, what they ate in their own huts and hovels, and what they loved first in a fight. That was the world, she thought. Ice at one corner, hot sand at another. That was the world: a patchwork you memorized for a test. That was the world—a spin of fire and smoke and wind and sweets to eat in the dark.

"Carol Ann," Eddie was saying.

He'd found her hand, and she, her heart a racket in her ears, could tell his question was coming now—would she move in with him? She had her answer ready, the words of it as simple as those the lucky would say in war.

After Valentine's Day, two weeks of living with him, she thought of the gun—Eddie's Makarov, scraped up from a field the LT had ordered cleared for horseshoes. She'd had a cold—the sniffles, chills occasionally—so she stayed home, faked a seal-like cough for Mr. Probert, then lay in bed all morning being serious with Donahue and Sally. At eleven, Geraldo came on—Centerfold Sisters, the girls blond and top-heavy and humorless as nuns—so at the commercial she shuffled into the kitchen for a cup of red zinger. She was at the cupboard when she realized it was still there: the pistol.

Eddie hoarded, nothing decrepit enough or useless enough or sufficiently broken to throw away. Everything, she realized, came with him: clothes, notes he'd scribbled to himself, a stack of *Times Heralds* from Dallas, shoes he'd scuffed the heels from, books he'd quit, letters and bills and cards from the kids. He'd made his way to her, she thought, gathering scraps and scraps of paper along the way—another trail—and, if she wanted, she could track backward through his life, the piles and mounds of it, until she came upon him at, say, fifteen—or five, or twenty—and see him there, clutched in his hand the first thing that marked the path he'd traveled through time.

In what had become his reading room—the third bedroom, already tiny and now cramped as an attic with cassettes and periodicals and accordion files—she sat in his chair, the footstool in front of it laden with catalogs and maps of places he'd, so far as she knew, never been to, places like France and mountainous Tibet, as remote and strange as lands you found in books about fairies and trolls and high-hatted wizards.

For a time, she toyed with the switch to the floor lamp. On and off. A cone of light over her shoulder, then a wash of morning as gray as the paint on warehouses. He'd stuck foil on several of the windows. A bulletin board dominated one wall, his customers scheduled in a grid that went till the new century. She was amused to see that he'd planned to be busy through 1999—the year, according to Mr. Probert, that Jesus, willful and heedless as a spendthrift, was returning to boil the mess that man was. She imagined Eddie then, over fifty, still lean as pricey meat, that figure beside him may be her own aged self in a dress too clever with snaps and buckles and bows to be anything but science fiction.

Eddie was an optimist, she decided. Every morning, he made lists—prune Mrs. Grissom's firebush, take down the shed at the Samples' house, get insecticide from the Mesilla Valley Garden Center—and he drove away in his pickup knowing what led to what and it to another until, at sundown, he could come back to this room to draw another X in his calendar. An X for then, an X for now. Xs enough for the future—maybe for jealous Jesus Himself—and whatever sob-filled hours came after that.

She sighed when she looked at the metal file cabinet underneath the grid. That's where it was, she thought. The gun. For a moment, laughter from the TV reaching her even here, she wondered what he would say if he knew she had opened a drawer, the top one, all squeaky and warped, and found it there, the barrel rust-flecked as she remembered, a web of cracks running up on the grip on one side. She was curious about how his face would work, the chewing movements of his mouth, if he knew that she'd held the pistol, absently rubbing the faded red star, studying the peculiar markings near the trigger guard, before she put it back— that squeak again—and went to see, as she was doing now, what opinions the Miss Septembers had regarding certain monkeyshines between girls and boys.

Once upon a time, she thought, Eddie had had a secret. Now she had one.

The end of February. March out like a lamb. Easter. He was fine for those months. May flowers. Then June, and he arrived for the class party on the last day straight from work—a new home he was landscaping in Telshor Hills, another big shot with a wallet like a loaf of bread. He ate a square of the spice sheetcake he'd baked the night before, drank Kool-Aid, even wore a party hat when Cheryl Lynn Baker—the smartie pants in the third row—pointed out the rules. Parties and hats went together like salt and pepper. Afterward, when she was cleaning up, he told her she could relax.

"It doesn't happen the way you think," he announced. "It's gradual."

He was sitting at her desk, smoking with deliberation, flicking ashes onto a paper plate.

Other rules, she guessed. Out the window, she could see some older kids—sixth graders, maybe Ruthie Evans's kids—gathered around the tetherball pole. It seemed probable that a fight would start out there. Or a powwow.

"It builds," he told her. "Something goes haywire. The waters rise."

In the hall, a bell was dinging: three-fifteeen. School had ended, officially.

"You're warning me," she said, a question. Another rule.

His shirt stained with sweat, a line of grit on his brow from his headband, he looked like a warrior who'd scrambled out of the hills for food.

"I fill up," he was saying. "It spills."

Outside, the sixth graders were wandering off in pairs or alone. Mr. Probert was out there, she assumed, fussy and loud as a drum. He looked like a man who'd removed his own sense of humor with a fork.

"You'll tell me when?" she asked.

Reaching for a fallen column of Dixie cups, he had stood, not hurriedly.

He'd clean up, he said. He'd tell her when.

For the Fourth of July, he took three days for them to visit her folks in Clovis. Since she'd left for college, her father had put in a pool, so he and Eddie sat under the awning on the cool deck drinking Pearl Light while she floated on a rubber raft near the diving board. Every now and then, she could hear them chuckling softly, then her Daddy teasing her mother who wouldn't leave the porch for the sun. "That water's cold as scissors," she said once. The light here was different—thinner somehow, less wrathful than in the desert—the landscape grassier, not so hardpan, but without jagged mountains at the horizon to show how far you had to go.

On the Fourth itself, they watched the fireworks from the city twelve miles south, miniature bursts of gold and green, like showers of foil, the sounds of the explosions arriving well after she'd seen the glitter against a sky black as the cape a witch wears.

"Incoming," Eddie remarked once, before taking her hand to let her know he was fooling. It had been like this in Vietnam, he told her father. A swimming pool, a porterhouse steak for each trooper, and an air force light show far, far away.

That night, after her parents had gone to bed, Carol Ann wished Eddie sweet dreams at the door to the guest bedroom where he was to sleep.

"They don't know," he said.

She couldn't see much of his face, just eerie glints from his cheek and nose. She hoped he was smiling.

"They're old-fashioned," she said. "Mother would be upset."

His hand came up then, out of the darkness, and reached into the cup of her swimsuit to hold her breast. He was dry, nothing in his touch to suggest that she was more to him than wood and nails and strings you could pull once or twice.

"You didn't tell me you had a nickname," he said. "Squeaky."

Laryngitis, she said. In grade school. It was, well, embarrassing. Sounded more like a frog than a mouse.

"You had a horse, too," he said. "Skeeter. It threw you out by the corral."

His hand was still there, unmoving. He could have been wearing a leather glove, and for a second she thought to go in the room with him, that she would shrug off her top and lie beside him until whatever was kicking at his heart ran out of anger.

"I like your parents," he told her. "They're straight shooters. You don't get much of that nowadays."

He had stopped smiling, she supposed. You could hear the earnestness in his voice, the sour note it was. She guessed he was thinking about the heroes he rooted for in the books he bought—books whose covers were all about doom and distress and deeds wrought by righteousness. In those books, shooting straight was a virtue. So far as she understood, the vices included hypocrisy and back stabbing. In Eddie's books, the characters suffered no fools. They rose up, indignant as children, and let fly with arrows and spears and lances.

"Eddie?" she said.

His hand had moved, like a claw. Down the hall, her father was coughing, a wheeze without any charm to it. She had been Squeaky once, she thought. She had been a Mobley, then a Spears. Now what? What were you in the dark? *One*. That had been Eddie's word months and months ago. What was one when the gears slipped or ground or disengaged completely?

It was happening, he said. Forewarned was forearmed.

3.

In early August, he stopped cooking. For several days he ate only peanut butter from the jar, then macaroni and cheese. He stared at the TV, yelled abuse at the gussied up newsfolk NBC had hired to educate him.

"You could see a doctor," she told him one evening.

"Only as a last resort," he said. It was like breathing through a soaked washcloth. They wrenched open your skull, dropped a torch in there, wriggled their fingers in the goo.

His hand was shaking in a fashion she suspected he was unaware of. It got better as you got older, he'd told her on the drive back from Clovis. He was getting older all the time.

"You're proud, aren't you?"

He smiled at her then, the whole of his face involved in the effort.

He was the King of Pride, he said. The absolute monarch.

On Thursday, the day his letter to the editor appeared in the *Sun-News*, he was working for Judge Sanders, putting in a rock and cactus garden, so she drove over to the park at the corner, far enough away to be inconspicuous. She'd seen the list—

ocotillo, monkey flower, brittle brush, gravel from an arroyo behind a mountain—his handwriting square and tight, as if written with a chisel.

They'd made love the night before—he only to her, she believed, but she to eight or nine of him. One of him had been feverish, another chilled enough to get goose bumps. One laughed, another whistled from the foot of the bed and lunged at her like a tiger, his head wagging heavily, his eyes dumb as marbles. The one in the refuge of the corner, knees to his chest, was not the one who rose from it, slow and shaggy-seeming. She hadn't been horrified, she thought now, recalling the steady thump of her heart. The lovemaking itself had been tedious: a matter of tabs and slots and careful movement. Eddie had been dry weight, all bone and ash—flesh that rocked back and forth regularly as clockwork. Once he sang along with his boombox—Patsy Cline, she remembered—but his voice had run out long before the music did, and when she lifted her face to look at him, she discovered that he was gone, the shell of him slick and unfeeling as glass.

"It's like a landslide," he said. "Imagine a hillside."

He was a shade, she'd thought. Insubstantial as a ghost. And for a time, astride him, trying to make him hard, she believed he was trying, in a way cockeyed with love, to protect her from the knowledge that life was not glorious and purposeful and prodigious with reward. They were a kind, he and she, dragged upright by time, but too addled to follow the generally forward direction thought best to go.

"Help me, Eddie," she said. "Please, help me."

He was trying, he said.

Again, she asked, but this time he said nothing, so she leaned into him, his smell at once bitter and greasy, salt and lemon and soap, her face against his neck, her lips to his ear, saying the word *love* with as much bite as she imagined a tyrant might say the word *kill*.

Much later—after she'd gone away, after he'd come back to himself—she realized this was the first time she'd told him she loved him, but it was a sentence she remembered cleaving to, like a monotonous beat, for one minute, then two, as pure and aggrieved the last time said as it was the first. The covers were in a knot at the foot of the bed; she grew cold as she spoke, the *I* of her pressed into the *you* of him, not knowing what she hoped to prove, then knowing—from his witless moans, from his hand stroking the small of her back—that she had everything to prove: he would be worse before he was better—Lordy, she understood that—but he had to know, even in the worst of it, that she loved him.

So she kept saying it, speech delivered into his neck and shoulder, to his cheeks and his forehead as she kissed him, into his chin when he smoothed back her hair, to his lips until he'd stopped trembling; and she was quiet, and it seemed that nothing—least of all sentiments having to do with the soul of her—had been said at all, until they reached a point in the night when he drew her to his chest to tell her to attend closely to the clatter and bang in him that were his various demons.

"I'm scared, Eddie," she said.

So was he, he told her. He was helpless.

On one wall, several shadows were at play from the candlelight, none of them meaningful or part of love.

"Tell me about the picture," she said. "The one Bobby made for you."

It was her spring formal, he said. She looked like ice cream to him. The only cool thing in the world. The LT, a West Point grad, had said Eddie's affection for it bordered on the inordinate.

"That was wrong," Eddie said. "My affection was as ordinate as the day is long."

Scarcely an inch apart, they lay side by side. Like an old couple, she thought. A modern schoolmarm and the King of Pride. She thought of her parents—Rilla and Cuddy—lying, probably like this, as distant from her as she seemed to be from Eddie. Once, when she was seven, she'd watched them nap, and she had tried, standing at the door to their bedroom, to imagine their dreams, wondering at last if, where in them it was dark and cool and broad as heaven, they dreamed themselves lying each by each, inert and almost breathless, no one but Carol Ann to beckon them back to the wakeful world.

"Let's go to sleep, Eddie," she'd said.

"Yes," he said, an answer with too much hiss in it.

"I love you," she'd said.

And he'd said it too, the dum-de-dum of it all she could remember between then and now, between Eddie looking as if his arms would fly off in agony and Eddie now bustling back and forth in the sun at Judge Sanders's house.

In her lap, she had the *Sun-News* open to the letters page. It was mid-August, school to start in three weeks, and already some lamebrains were writing to complain about a teachers' strike Carol Ann didn't think would actually happen. At home, reading his letter had frightened her, but here, only a half-block from him, she tried again, saying aloud the first paragraph—it was long as her forearm—until her eyes came free of the page and she could see that Eddie was stock-still at the door to his pickup, his head cocked back, the sky blank and almost white behind him. Edward L. Heber, the letter writer, was not a lunatic. Edward L. Heber was angry. *Things are out of whack*, he'd written. *Collapsed and ruined. There is hunger. And ignorance. And false piety. And*—but she'd stopped again, Eddie with a broom now, leaning on it and again looking upward.

He was a moralist, she decided. Maybe that was good. A hopey thing with wings.

For another twenty minutes she watched him work, the yardage between them filled only with heat shimmering up from the asphalt. Load after load, he was shoveling out gravel, carrying it to a pile near the walk leading to the Judge's front door. Clearly, this was how he managed—one simple undertaking at a time: scoop, walk, dump, everything about his manner calculated and efficient, as if he could do this, happily and well, until he found himself at the bottom of a pit, alone at last with the one stone that had made him furious. She tried to conceive of the inside of his head—the fountain of sparks in there, the rattle—but a second later she realized he had stopped, in mid-stride almost, as fixed as a scarecrow. Something significant was about to happen.

"What're you doing here?" he asked.

Still carrying the shovel, he had taken only a half minute to reach her—she'd timed it. Amazingly, he had not dropped even one pebble.

"I don't know," she said. "I should be over at school, but—" She shrugged. What with the union yakking about the strike, she didn't see any wisdom in fixing up her classroom if in a week she was going to be walking a picket line and generally making a fool of herself. "I thought we could go out to dinner tonight," she said. "Maybe a movie after."

It was blabber. What she really wanted to do was grab his sleeve, make him leave the shovel here, the truck there, and get in the car with her. They would sit for a while, another lovelorn couple in paradise. She would hold his hand—or he the heft of hers—the afternoon would wear on, dusk would arrive, then twilight, then night itself full of random twinkles or a moon on the wane.

"I made a call," he said. "This morning."

Before she understood completely what he'd done, she sought to rewind time, yank the cord of it back so that he was not here, beside her window. She yearned to be young again, the ideas of fate and circumstance as alien to her as were orchids to Eskimos.

"Bobby Spears," she said, a statement of fact, like the number of bushels in a peck.

The shovel jerked now, a handful of gravel spilling.

"He's got an extra room," Eddie said. "You'll be safe there."

Her lungs filled then—a gasp, nearly—and she feared Eddie would be turning now, going away, back to his work, back to the truck, back to the thirty-two steps between it and the mountain he had contrived to erect in the front yard of a retired Muny Court judge. He was trying to protect her again. Maybe that was good, too.

"Don't be mad, Carol Ann," he said. "I don't know anybody else."

"What about the girlfriend?" she asked.

They were married, Eddie told her. The girl—Sally or something—she was pregnant. Bobby was different.

"This seemed like a smart idea, Eddie?"

He only had one card left, he said. He'd played it.

On the seat next to her, the paper was still open, the rage and sorrow of Edward Lonnie Heber not anything any citizen would remember tomorrow, or the days to follow. Elsewhere were articles about mayhem and conniving and the snapped-off ends of hope. *We are craven*, Eddie had instructed the neighbors, and the neighbors' neighbors, and anyone else who could read left to right. *We must mend. Now.*

"How long?" Carol Ann wondered.

He didn't know, he said. Six weeks maybe, more or less. It's been quite a while since the last episode.

She thought about last night, watching his sleep, the peace it had seemed to bring him, then her own sleep, nothing but wire in her dreams—fists of it, huge coils sprung and bent and twisted—then awake and seeing him frozen in the hall, the light a glare in front of him, his face shriven and woeful, a scary amount of time going by before he shivered to life again and stumbled toward her.

"I'll give you a month," she said. "I couldn't last any longer."

"Okay," he said, little in the word to indicate it had any meaning for him. "I gotta go back to work, Carol Ann."

"Okay," she said, her turn not to mean too much.

He moved then, the shovel a counterweight to keep him from falling over in a heap. His tattoo had come into view, crude and obviously unfinished, the handiwork of a B&E offender named Ike. Sometimes, Eddie wore a bandage to cover it. He was ashamed, he'd told her long ago. A dragon, he'd sneered. How corny.

"Eddie," she called.

More gravel fell.

"What'd you see last night?" she asked. "In the hall."

He told her then, but she believed she hadn't heard correctly, so she asked him to repeat himself—"Fire," he said, the way "sin" is said in wonderland. And while he walked away, she thought she could see it, too, the yellow and red of it roaring up and up, and the terrifying wind of it overtaking everything in front of her—the trees, these houses, the telephone poles, shrubs, Eddie's truck, at last Eddie himself—until all that remained was rubble scorched black as a nightmare.

4.

She guessed that he cracked—caved in completely—her second week on the picket line in front of her school. She had not gone to Bobby's house—"it would be too complicated," she'd told Sally, Bobby's pretty wife; instead, she rented a furnished efficiency in a four-plex Mr. Probert owned up the valley toward Hot Springs, a place where she learned, the instant the door shut behind her, that a day could have too many hours in it, an hour too many minutes, time as mixed and fluid and dreadful a dimension as that found in cartoons. She awoke too early, she discovered. Stayed up too late, darkness a thing that seemed to have texture and depth.

The first few days, she didn't eat much. Once, she almost fainted on the line, so each morning thereafter, before her shift, she made breakfast—a bowl of Cheerios, toast and jelly, a glass of grapefruit juice—and sat in front of it with that promise that she would do this—and the next chore, plus whatever ought to follow that—and then, for one creaky turn of the planet at least, she would not have to do it again. Often as she ate, she wondered what Eddie was doing, the idea of him so urgent and so potent that sometimes he appeared across from her, his hair gleaming, his face soaking up most of the light she needed to see by.

Several times she called, his machine clicking on to say he was not in. He'd bought a gag tape—the voices of Daffy Duck and Bogart and Ronald Reagan—and twice, aiming to be cheerful, she left messages in the style of Marilyn Monroe and Yosemite Sam. The last time she told him the gossip she was hearing—Rae Nell Tipton was divorcing Archie, the slime; Mavis Rugely had a goiter—but she quickly ran out of silly news and, the tape whirring like a breeze, she suspected he was squatting near the phone, his own cigarette going, a comforter over his shoulders to keep him from coldness no one else in Dona Ana County could feel.

"Go to bed, Eddie," she said softly. "Put the beer down, honey. You need rest."

She imagined him shuffling back to the bedroom, all the lights on so he could see the winged creatures in the night that had swooped down to scold him. "Lie down," she told him, and when she assumed he was settled, the covers clutched to his neck, she began to talk to him again, hers the voice she used at school when it was time for naps and dreams fine as mist. They would go places, she promised him. Canada. Niagra Falls. Florida. If he wanted, he could invite his kids. They'd rent a van, maybe a Winnebago, and in the summers they'd drive all over America. She'd camped a lot, she reminded him. She knew the forest. Plus, she liked to climb, the steeper the better, get to the peak of a mountain and shout into the valley you'd left. "I'm a good sport," she said, listening closely. He wasn't asleep, she thought. He remained alert there, still vigilant, his gaze as watchful as a stray dog ready to run.

"It's okay, sweetheart," she said and took enough breath to start again on the list of vistas to visit and adventures to share.

The next day, she thought she saw his truck a ways down the block from the sidewalk she marched up and down on, but she couldn't be sure: Kirby Holmes, the loudmouth from the classroom next to hers, was telling another of his Cajun jokes—a sing-songy anecdote with too many wishy-washy characters in it and about nothing life-or-death that could actually happen between men and women. She became distracted—Kirby was jumping around and making her look here and there—and suddenly what might have been Eddie Heber, maybe standing beside his pickup, his wave constant and spiritless, was only emptiness, just a street that went up and up and finally over a hill, a curve going on and on into the sterile and wild desert.

He had cracked—she knew it—so that night she drove over to his house. "Oh, Eddie," she sighed, as much exasperated as heartsick. All the lights were on—inside and out, as far as she could tell—the place a glow she figured the cops might worry over. After she used her key to get in, she suppressed the impulse to turn around, to close up the house again, and disappear.

"Eddie," she called.

A tornado had torn through there, it seemed, and she wondered where in the litter of tipped-over furniture and strewn paper and crumpled clothes she would find him. "It's me, baby," she said, then again and again until she tired of the echo.

Cautiously, she picked her way through the living room, magazines like stepping-stones laid out by a child. He'd been drinking Coors, she noticed, at least a case of empty cans stacked in a lopsided pyramid beside his chair, and for a moment she presumed to smell him, the sand he brought home in his jeans, oil and gasoline from his mowers, the sticky goop trees left on his shirt. In the next moment, she made a lot of noise—coughing, slamming the door—the hopeful half of her certain that he would rush out of the bedroom now, or the bathroom, and lead her somewhere by the hand as he had the first time she'd come here; but she could see the holes in the plaster board, the hammer plunged in a gash near the kitchen entry—dozens and dozens of holes, precise and in a pattern she suspected would only be awful from over a mile away—and she knew that Edward Lonnie Heber had lost his ability, miraculous as magic, to appear in her life out of thin air.

In the kitchen, she found the knife on the counter, its blade crusty with dried blood. Next to it was a smeared hand print—three fingers and the heel of his palm. Another smudge. And a third, droplets spattered against the back splash and on the floor tile leading yonder. Her heart in her throat like a squirrel, all claws and climbing, she told herself to calm down. "An accident," she insisted and after another moment to believe it, insisted it again—and followed the splatters down the hall to the bathroom where the sink was splotched with prints and speckles of blood, the medicine cabinet door hanging open. He'd had an accident, she thought. He'd gotten out iodine, Mercurochrome, and Curad bandages, the box of adhesive tape ripped apart as if he'd attacked it with his teeth. From the tub, she picked up a towel matted with more blood. He had been crazy. And bleeding. And bending over here to—what?

Sitting on the edge of the tub, she thought hard about not thinking even one little bit. "Be calm," she told herself.

Later, when he came home and she could see he'd tried to cut out the tattoo on his arm, she told him she'd run throughout the house then, out of thoughts to think, at once furious and miserable. She opened every door, even the closets, the numbest parts of her convinced he'd fled into one and she'd find him curled on the floor, unconscious in a nest of shoes and workboots, only the body of him left to holler at or pound on.

She went into the backyard, she told him, into the utility room at the back of the carport and looked behind the stockade fence he'd built to hide the garbage cans from the street. She told him what her heart was doing, the ragged riot it was making, and how quickly she'd run out of breath and that she'd stubbed her toe in his study when she'd seen his Xs had stopped, all of them; and that she'd sat only when she played back his messages, hearing voice after tinny voice, men and women alike—some fretful, a few downright offensive—asking where the hell he was or would he come on Wednesday; and then came her own voice, whispery and strained, at the instant she spotted his note to her on his wall calendar, a little girl's voice almost that asked him to call her, to say he was all right, that she missed him, even as she read his note once, then twice, then a third time before the sentences, clearly too ordinary to be only about him and her, made sense: "It's bad," he'd written. "I'm checking myself in. Don't know how long. I knew you'd come."

Somewhere a car horn was blasting. It seemed endless, noisy as news from hell. I can wait, she told herself.

In the morning, she called Ruthie. She had not slept, she thought, though she did remember snapping up rigid and saucer-eyed three or four times from a dense and muddled state akin to sleep. She had been dropping down a hole, the bottom hurtling up silently to catch her.

"I'm going to have to skip my shift," she said.

"No problem," Ruthie said. "You'll miss Rae Nell's celebration, though. The ice cream man's supposed to come by, union treat."

Ruthie went on—harmless chitchat about Rae Nell's separation, plus Mr. Probert's scowling at the pickets from his office window—but Carol Ann could not listen.

Dawn had come up sparkling and sharp, the destruction around her plain to even the most innocent eye. She was being evaluated, she felt, and the image of a big book—an old-timey ledger of a book, sizable enough for the paws of Goliath himself—had heaved into view. A hand seemed poised over a newly turned page and ready to begin the burdensome process of recording about her what had been true and not.

"It could be a while," she said. "You shouldn't count on me."

"You sick, Carol Ann?" Ruthie asked. "You sound pukey."

She considered what Eddie had left her, a whole year to keep her occupied. She had been drunk, she felt, all life's elements—the mineral included—beautifully sensible now that the fog had cleared between her ears. She would clean, she had decided.

"Personal business," she said. "Eddie says howdy."

After the first room, she developed a rhythm, playing a game in her mind to keep from crawling into bed and tugging the bedspread over her head for a year. *A is for apple*, she thought. *B is for bedlam*. And she kept going—*D* was for *diminish*, *M* for *madness*—turning around at the end of the alphabet to get to *A* by talking backward; then around again—*C* was for *caliph*, *F* for *fool*—like a shuttle back and forth until she could shut a door behind her and announce to the well-mopped floors and the well-scrubbed walls that she was done, done, done. One day she went by *N* seven times—*naughty, nice, nasty, neat, nether, nonce, nifty*—the next day *P*, as in *pail*. As in *prayer*.

While she worked, she played his boombox—the Rascals, Simon and Garfunkel—keeping the music low so she would hear the phone when it rang. In the evening, she exercised with the barbell she'd uncovered in the storeroom by the Weber grill, and toward midnight, after her shower, she wrote letters on the portable Olivetti Eddie used for his monthly statements. "Dear Bobby," she typed, congratulating him on his marriage, on what a lovely wife Sally seemed to be, and wishing him good fortune with his new baby. In too many pages, she explained their life together. They were young, she wrote him. Babies themselves. They couldn't know what might make them joyful. She stopped, nothing between her brain and the keyboard but hands that seemed strange as boots on cows.

The next letter went to Eddie's kids, in care of their mother. "I am Carol Ann Mobley," she began. "I used to be a teacher." They were children, she remembered, the oldest—Eric, the towhead—no more than a seventh grader, so she put down only those features of her character that they wouldn't be disappointed to discover on their own. "I am a Democrat," she wrote. "Except squash, I like most vegetables. I love your father very much. I oppose disloyalty and cheating. Maybe next summer we can meet, go to Yellowstone." She saw them in the wilderness, like pioneers, self-sufficient and content to feast upon the bounty nature sent them. They had a house, hewn from timbers Eddie had harvested. They bathed in streams, walked the hills and dales they owned. In the evening, after dinner, they stood in a circle, holding hands and looking upward to whatever eye was looking down.

That evening, the last letter went to Milton E. Probert, Principal: "I quit," she wrote, adding the word *respectfully* above her signature before crossing it out. Respect had become irrelevant. As had duty and work life and civility, all the notions that made the past the past.

"Don't give the children to Kirby Holmes," she printed on the envelope after she sealed it. "He's a jerk and a show-off."

His call came later in September while she was wishing for rain, a sooty sky of it, a grade of weather from the meaner verses of the Bible.

"It's you," she said. The letter the night before—"The last of the last," she'd told one wall she'd become pals with—had been to her parents. *I am getting married*, she'd written. *The man you met last summer. He's sick now, but he'll be well soon. Expect us for Christmas.* "Where are you?"

The VA unit, he said. William Beaumont Hospital at Fort Bliss.

"That's in El Paso," she said. "I know that."

His reply had been toneless, impersonal as a suit, as if he'd been taught to talk by spacemen.

"I could drive down," she said. "A visit."

She didn't know how, but she could tell he was shaking his head, and after a few seconds it came, his *no*. He was in tough shape, he admitted. They'd given him stuff, the medics. Drugs. His face had puffed up. He looked like a pumpkin, he said. A moment passed—time like a house haunted and ramshackle enough to lose your way in—before she realized he'd made a joke.

"I called your customers," she told him. "You're in California, they think, a family emergency. Most of them understood."

She had more to say—that, in fact, she'd mown several lawns herself, that she'd learned how to run the weed-whacker, that she'd even cut down an upright willow with black leaf disease. Many, many days had passed, she wanted him to know, and she was a quick study, but he was talking again, words coming to her as if they'd come to him down a pipe from heaven, punctuation a courtesy only necessary to the crawling ugly order of beasts, little to suggest she wasn't listening to an angel, infernal as a machine, that could only chatter at top speed.

"Slow down, baby," she said.

Here it was that he told he'd cut his hair. "It's a butch," he said. "I look in the mirror, there's a ghoul."

She remembered him as he'd been when they met—years and years ago. An eon, it seemed. There had been people—ghouls themselves no doubt. Games had been played. She could remember laughter, throaty and barking. Arms and legs and hips and corners to round, shouts that became hoots, the music of horns, all brassy and clanging like sheets of metal, and always his eyes fixed on her, no matter where she was. It was like thinking about the age of dinosaurs and bogs, the world too wet and smoky and hot to support any animals except those pea-brained and ponderous, a time of bruise-like skies and churning, molten seas when humankind was not yet even mud.

"I'm forty-one," he said. "I'm supposed to live another thirty years."

Something had ended, she realized. Something new had begun.

"Eddie," she said, "what were you doing? Before you came to school that day—all those months before you took me home?"

His answer had no consequence, she thought. They had it, the pistol. It was Russian, she recalled. Mar-something. Or Mak-. In that drawer, the screechy battered drawer. She'd held it again, light as a book you could read in an hour. It had once been Eddie's; now it seemed to be hers. Whatever. It was there—useful or not.

He'd been following her, he was saying. There were probably laws against that now.

"I-Beam was mustering his courage," she suggested, his nickname from that other era.

By the same instinct of heart and happenstance that earlier she had known he was shaking his head *no*, she believed now that he was nodding *yes*, and for a second she imagined following herself as he had. Carol Ann in pursuit of Carol Ann. Seeing how crummy and humdrum her life had been. Pointing to the ruts she'd worn in the world, the lines she would not cross. And then, his courage mustered, Eddie had caught up with her, as she was doing now.

"When I was little," she told him, "I wanted to be someone else."

He knew the feeling, he said. Another joke without much ha-ha in it.

"A girl you read about in a magazine," she said. "With red hair. A ballerina. I could make her up and be her, Eddie. My voice changed. I had green eyes and could speak the most fluent French. Her name was Sabrina."

He liked it, he said. Sounded exotic.

Sitting at the kitchen table, the phone like a weight against her ear, she understood she had only a fixed amount of conversation left. Only a dozen words—possibly fewer—none of them less precious than gold or likewise goodies from the vault of Ali Baba himself. In the background she heard hospital noises, goblins and haints and spirits on the loose, and Eddie's breathing in the foreground like waves washing rocks. Only a few more words, she thought, then she could lie in the tub, the water to her chin, perhaps a glass of wine handy, and not know how the next minute would turn out.

"Come home, baby," she said. "Sabrina says come home."

Leo Tolstoy

While poring over past issues of STORY *we found this gem by Leo Tolstoy. Whit Burnett published "A Child's Garden of Morals" in the Summer, 1948 issue and wrote these accompanying notes:*

"Josephine B. Embury of New York recently discovered that Tolstoy had written a number of little moral tales for his children which had so far not been translated into English. A student of many languages, she set to work to translate them and here are presented three that demonstrate the great novelist in one of his moral and fatherly roles. It was Tolstoy's idea that art in which the simplest feelings are made accessible to all (such as folk legends, songs and tales) tends to unite mankind."

We agree. And we present these three fables once again as a timeless encore.

A Child's Garden of Morals

LEO TOLSTOY

The Old Grandfather and the Grandson

The grandfather had become very old. His legs wouldn't go, his eyes didn't see, his ears didn't hear, he had no teeth. And when he ate, the food dripped from his mouth.

The son and daughter-in-law stopped setting a place for him at the table and gave him supper in back of the stove. Once they brought dinner down to him in a cup. The old man wanted to move the cup and dropped and broke it. The daughter-in-law began to grumble at the old man for spoiling everything in the house and breaking the cups and said that she would now give him dinner in a dishpan. The old man only sighed and said nothing.

Once the husband and wife were staying at home and watching their small son playing on the floor with some wooden planks: he was building something. The father asked: "What is it that you are doing, Misha?" And Misha said: "Dear Father, I am making a dishpan. So that when you and dear Mother become old, you may be fed from this dishpan."

The husband and wife looked at one another and began to weep. They became ashamed of so offending the old man, and from then on seated him at the table and waited on him.

The Jump

A ship had been making a tour around the world and was on its way home. The weather was calm; everyone was on deck. In the crowd of people a large monkey was whirling around and entertaining everyone. Jumping, making funny faces, contorting itself and mimicking, the monkey knew it was droll and therefore became still more inspired.

It hopped up to a twelve-year-old boy, son of the ship's captain, plucked the hat off his head, put it on, and quickly climbed up the mast. Everyone began to laugh, but the boy was left without a hat and didn't know whether to be amused or angry.

The monkey sat on the first crossbeam of the mast, took off the hat, and began to tear it to pieces with its teeth and paws. As if to provoke the boy, it displayed the hat to him and made faces.

The boy shouted and threatened it, but it still wickedly tore the hat. The sailors began to laugh more loudly, but the boy became red in the face, threw off his jacket, and rushed up the mast after the monkey. In a minute he had climbed over the rope to the first crossbeam, but the monkey, even more skillfully and faster than he, climbed still higher at the instant the boy tried to grab the hat.

"You cannot escape me like that," shouted the boy.

The monkey again beckoned him, climbing still higher, but the boy was really angered and continued to climb. So within a minute the monkey and the boy had reached the very top. The monkey stretched itself out and hooked the crossbeam with the back of its hand, hung up the hat on the end of the next crossbeam, climbed to the top of the mast, and from there contorted its body and showed its teeth gleefully.

From the mast to the end of the crossbeam where the hat was hanging, it was two long steps, so that it was impossible for the boy to reach the hat without letting go of the mast and rope with his hands.

But the boy was very angry. He let go of the mast and stepped on to the crossbeam. On the deck everyone was looking and laughing at the amusement provided by the monkey and the captain's son, but as they saw him release the rope and step on the crossbeam, balancing with his hands, they all became frozen with fear.

One slip and he would be smashed to pieces upon the deck. But even if he were not to slip, to reach the edge of the crossbeam and seize the hat would make it difficult for him to retrace his steps and reach the mast.

Everybody was silently watching him and waiting to see what would happen.

Suddenly someone in the crowd groaned from fear. The boy collected himself when he heard this cry, looked down, and wavered.

Just then, the captain of the ship, the boy's father, came out of his cabin. He was carrying a gun to shoot seagulls. He saw his son on the mast and immediately aimed at him, shouting: "Into the water! Jump right away into the water! I will shoot!" The boy hesitated but didn't understand. "Jump, or I will shoot! One, two—" and as soon as the father shouted "three," the boy lowered his head and jumped.

The body of the boy hit the water with a splash like a cannon ball, but before the waves had time to fully cover him, twenty young sailors leaped from the ship. Within a few seconds that seemed long to everyone, the boy came up to the surface. He was grabbed and hauled to safety. Water poured from his nose and mouth and he breathed again.

When the captain saw this he suddenly cried out as if something oppressed him and ran back to his own cabin, so that nobody could see how bitterly he was weeping.

The Swans

A flock of swans was flying from cold shores to warm lands. They were flying across the sea. They flew day and night, and from one day to the following night, they flew, not resting, over the water.

In the sky was a full moon, and the swans saw in the distance, far down under them, a little blue water. All the swans were tired to death flapping their wings, but they took no rest and continued to fly. In front flew the strong old swans; behind flew the younger and more delicate.

One young swan was flying behind all the others. His strength gave out. He beat his wings and couldn't fly any further. Spreading out his wings he went down closer and closer to the water, but his comrades beyond went on, further and further, shimmering white in the light of the moon.

The swan alighted on the water and folded up his wings. The sea rocked under him. The flock of swans was still visible on the white horizon line of the sky. And the whirring of their wings could hardly be heard in the silence. When they were shut off entirely from view, the swan bent his neck back and shut his eyes. He didn't stir and only the sea lifted and lowered him.

Before daybreak a gentle breeze began to rock the sea. And the water lapped at the white breast of the swan. The swan opened his eyes. In the east the dawn glowed, and the moon and the stars grew paler. The swan breathed again, stretching out his neck and flapping his wings, raised himself a little and flew, his wings still clinging to the water. Higher and higher he lifted himself and when the water was far below him he flew toward the shores where the warm lands lay. Alone, over mysterious waters, he flew to where his comrades before him had flown.

— Translated by Josephine B. Embury

LEE K. ABBOTT is the author of five collections of stories, most recently *Living After Midnight* (Putnam, 1991). He teaches at the Ohio State University in Columbus.

"Like so many of my stories, 'The Way Sin Is Said in Wonderland' came to me from a voice—maybe from my unconscious or maybe from one of those angels we as a fallen kind are said to have as guardians. Less mysteriously, the story has something to do with an incident early in my tenure as a writer at Case Western Reserve University in Cleveland, where, among my students, I had one who was especially crazy and brilliant.

"I visited this young man—who has, notwithstanding his troubles, accumulated MA and MFA degrees and is now in law school—at the Hannah Pavilion, a mental hospital, where toward the end of my visit he took me into his room to blow soap bubbles from a cup and to warn me that the CIA was listening to him through the smoke alarms on the ceiling. Earlier, he had played me a song, written in my honor, on his guitar. That evening, he said, he was going to play onstage with the Grateful Dead. He would sneak out, he'd said. The world needed to hear from him.

"Like my Eddie, he was outraged and scornful, reckless and proud. Like my Carol Ann, I was intrigued and smitten. And I suppose the pages you've read are all about what it must be like to love such a person, or what in our own selves Eddie is the incarnation of, who is so righteous and driven and mad."

CHARLES D'AMBROSIO's "A Christmas Card" marks his second appearance in STORY. "Jacinta" was published in the Winter 1992 issue.

"This little piece began with snow, some baroque music, and the book of Isaiah, where a six-winged seraphim comes to the prophet and puts a hot coal on his lips, talking away his iniquity and giving him the power of speech. A hot coal would have been silly, so I used a hot potato. It happens that Isaiah is one of my mom's favorite books in the Bible, so I made my character have trouble saying what Christmas was like to *his* mother. The traditional celebration, I felt, was all cockeyed and slanty. There are three wise men in the Bible, of course, and I have some brothers, one of whom got his head blotted out, although not with a snowflake."

SUSAN JANE GILMAN recently completed the MFA program at the University of Michigan. Her fiction has appeared in *Ploughshares* and *The Village Voice*, her journalism in *The New York Times*, *Newsday* and *The New York Observer*, among other newspapers.

"When I was ten, my mother took our family to learn transcendental meditation. My brother and I were mortified at the prospect, particularly when we were required to donate a week's allowance to the Maharishi. To make us more amenable to meditating, the people at the meditation center invited us to a 'children's TM Christmas party.' Yet most of the other children who were meditating were doing so because they were diagnosed as hyperactive. Halfway through the Christmas party, their Ritalin wore off, and the party turned into a free-for-all. Years later, this struck me as an interesting scene for a story."

PAULA K. GOVER was born and raised in the center of Michigan's lower peninsula, and received her MFA in 1987 from the University of Michigan, where she was granted four Avery Hopwood Fellowships, including three first-place awards in poetry. Her poetry and fiction have appeared in *MS.*, *Framework*, *Calyx*, *The Seattle Review*, *Crosscurrents*, *The Southern Review*, and *The Virginia Quarterly Review*. *VQR* selected her story "White Boys and River Girls" as their 1992 Balch Award winner, and the story will also appear in the 1993 edition of *New Stories from the South*. Her collection of short fiction *A Woman Like Me* is forthcoming from Algonquin, and she is currently working on a novel. At present, Paula lives with her son, Aaron Gover, in Mt. Pleasant, Michigan.

"While I've moved fourteen times within the past thirteen years, every third or fourth year I've drifted back to Michigan again. As the state's geography and seasons are dramatic in and of themselves, it's impossible to imagine not reflecting these elements within my work. 'The Kid's Been Called Nigger Before' is swept with snow from start to finish, yet the story originated with a single image, and one which insisted on hope beyond the winds of a cruel storm front. Life has been tough for the story's three characters, and has become even tougher in the wake of new conflict brought about by a family gathering. Skating along the highway in an ill-running car, each character is struggling alone to put life back in order, and not sure what needs to be said or done. The story might have gone off in a different direction, but the closing image has always returned to the point at which I first began: they are going home."

KNICKERBOCKER (a.k.a. Nicholas Blechman) works as a graphic artist in New York, where he edits and publishes an underground comics magazine, *Nozone*. His illustrations have appeared in *The New York Times*, *The Guardian* and *The National Lampoon*.

"Genetic manipulation and freakish weather patterns linked to atmospheric pollution fueled this prophetic fairy tale of absurdity and loss of control. Television, arbiter of truth and in continual denial of the actual state of things, here becomes the ultimate element of absurdity."

MAX PHILLIPS is a graphic designer living and working in New York City. His stories have appeared in publications ranging from *The Antioch Review* to *The Village Voice*, and he has recently received an NEA Fellowship and a Paul Engle Fellowship.

"In 1987 I took part in a protest much like the one in this story. It was neither my first nor my last antinuclear action, but I was in an oddly suggestible frame of mind. I was preparing to leave my native city, New York, for good. (Or so I thought.) I was preparing to quit my profession, graphic design, for good. (Or so I thought.) My personal belongings were in boxes and my personal life had disintegrated with a noise like a watermelon striking a concrete floor — something between a thud and a squelch. I was thirty years old and felt three times that age. When I wrote 'Nevertheless,' I compromised and made Dean sixty-three.

"There was something weirdly comforting about addressing troubles much vaster than one's own, and I wanted to write about that. I also wanted to mention, for those who think peace activism went out with mood rings, that neither the danger of nuclear war nor the response to that danger has quite faded away."

STEVEN RINEHART was raised in Europe and Illinois, educated in Hawaii and Iowa, and lives in New York City. His fiction has appeared in several quarterlies, including *The Georgia Review*, *Black Warrior Review*, and *The Hawaii Review*. He is currently at work on a play.

"Three things came together to create 'Burning Luv.' One was the sight of a smoldering pickup truck alongside the interstate in downtown Oakland, a few weeks after the earthquake. Elvis Presley was playing on the radio and thus that truly awful pun of a title was born and wouldn't go away. Another was the conviction that what the world really needed was another psychotic hitchhiker story. The third was an uneasy feeling in my moral center when I allowed a despicable character to survive my novel unscathed and unrepentant. 'Burning Luv' more or less describes that character's eventual comeuppance."

ELIZABETH SPENCER is the author of twelve works of fiction, including *Jack of Diamonds* (a collection of five novellas) and, her most recent novel, *The Night Travellers* (both from Viking Penguin). Born and raised in Mississippi, she spent five years in Italy and lived until recently in Montreal. In her fiction, she has drawn on both these places as well as on the South for setting and character. In 1986 she moved with her husband John Rusher to Chapel Hill, North Carolina.

" 'The Weekend Travellers' stems from a time when my husband and I were often just that in short trips to New England. We once stumbled upon a rather sinister pottery shop like the one in the story, where we quickly bought a plate and left. While the two people and their adventure are fictional, I have noted that the New England landscape, though beguiling and lovely, can suddenly turn strangely haunted. The plate is still in my cupboard."

SYLVIA WATANABE's first book, *Talking to the Dead*, a collection of short fiction, was published by Doubleday in 1992. It was a finalist for the PEN/Faulkner award.

"My mother died a few years ago, and I remain haunted by the experience. I originally wrote 'Where People Know Me' as a kind of nonfiction account when I was approached by Mickey Pearlman to contribute to an anthology of essays on friendship called *Between Friends* that she was editing for Houghton Mifflin. As I worked on the piece, I became more aware than ever of the ways in which the narrative structure transforms what it tells, and of the difference between fiction and nonfiction as one of language and convention. Curiously, after completing the essay, I felt a vague dissatisfaction because it was not enough a *story*. And that is how the version here came about."

JOY WILLIAMS has written three novels, *State of Grace*, *The Changeling*, and *Breaking and Entering*, as well as two collections of stories, *Taking Care* and *Escapes*, available through Vintage Contemporaries. Her essays on hunting and the environment have appeared in *The Best American Essays* anthologies. She was recently awarded the Strauss Living Award from the American Academy of Arts and Letters. She lives in Key West.

"I've often thought about D.H. Lawrence's comment about the essential American soul being 'hard, isolate, stoic and a killer. It is never yet melted.' This story isn't the one I wanted to write actually, but I'm pleased with this little girl."

GLIMMER TRAIN STORIES

Northwest Short-Story Award for New Writers

PRIZES: $1200, publication of story in Fall 1994 GTS, and 20 copies of that issue, to winner. First/second runners-up will receive $500/$300, respectively, and honorable mention.

OPEN TO: Writers whose fiction has not appeared in a nationally-distributed publication.

WHAT TO SEND: A copy of your original (1200-6000 word) story, $10 reading fee, cover letter with your name, address, and the words "NW Short-Story Award for New Writers".

IMPORTANT DETAILS: Must be postmarked between Feb. 1 and March 31, 1994. No more than two stories per entry, and must be sent in the same envelope. Materials will not be returned, so no need for SASE. We cannot acknowledge receipt or provide status of any particular manuscript. Send SASE for guidelines.

ANNOUNCEMENT OF WINNERS: All applicants receive the Fall 1994 issue, in which winner and runners-up will be announced.

Glimmer Train Press NW Short-Story Award for New Writers,
812 SW Washington St., #1205, Portland, OR 97205.

STORY Back Issues

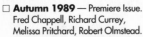

Complete your STORY collection with future literary classics for only $5.

1992 National Magazine Award for Fiction

- ☐ **Autumn 1989** — Premiere Issue. Fred Chappell, Richard Currey, Melissa Pritchard, Robert Olmstead.
- ☐ **Spring 1990** — Rick Bass, Hortense Calisher, Charles Baxter, Hilding Johnson.
- ☐ **Summer 1990** — Charlotte Holmes, Rick DeMarinis, Bobbie Ann Mason, Rachel Simon.
- ☐ **Autumn 1990** — Alice Adams, Alice Schell, Kate Braverman.
- ☐ **Winter 1991** — Joyce Carol Oates, Pamela Painter, Annette Sanford, Tom Chiarella.
- ☐ **Spring 1991** — Antonya Nelson, Madison Smartt Bell, William Kotzwinkle, Annick Smith.
- ☐ **Summer 1991** — Edward Allen, Melanie Sumner, William deBuys, Steven Millhauser.
- ☐ **Spring 1992** — Pamela Painter, Ron Carlson, Barbara Gowdy, Mary Bush.
- ☐ **Summer 1992** — Amy Bloom, Daniel Wallace, Candyce Barnes, Robert Siegel.

Please check the issues you want, cut out this order form, and mail it in with your check or money order to: STORY Back Issues, 1507 Dana Avenue, Cincinnati, Ohio 45207. Back issues are $5 per issue (includes postage and handling). Outside U.S. send $8.50 per issue and remit in U.S. funds. Ohio residents enclose 5.5% sales tax.

Total Amount Enclosed_____

Name_____

Address_____

City_____

State _____ Zip _____

STAD

CLASSIFIEDS

GRANTS/FELLOWSHIPS
LET THE GOVERNMENT FINANCE your career in writing. Free recorded message. (707)448-0200. (5LL1)

PRINTING/TYPESETTING

TAPES
MASTERING PROCRASTINATION & WRITER'S BLOCK. . . Psycho-Analytically Oriented Audio Tape . . . dedicated to Mastering Time & Creativity. $12.95. Louis Birner, Ph.D., P.O. Box 2A, 823 Park Ave., New York, NY 10021.

STATEMENT OF OWNERSHIP, MANAGEMENT AND CIRCULATION (Required by Act of August 12, 1970: Section 3685, Title 39, United States Code). STORY is published quarterly at 1507 Dana Avenue, Cincinnati, Ohio 45207. The general business offices of the publishers are located at 1507 Dana Avenue, Cincinnati, Ohio 45207. The general business offices of the publisher and editor are: Publisher, Richard Rosenthal, 1507 Dana Avenue, Cincinnati, Ohio 45207; Editor, Lois Rosenthal, 1507 Dana Avenue, Cincinnati, Ohio 45207. The owner is F&W Publications, Inc.: Richard Rosenthal, President. Address: 1507 Dana Avenue, Cincinnati, Ohio 45207. The extent and nature of circulation is: A. Total number of copies printed (Net press run). Average number of copies each issue during preceding 12 months 31,909. Actual number of copies of single issue published nearest to filing date 34,500. B. Paid circulation. 1. Sales through dealers and carriers, street vendors and counter sales. Average number of copies each issue during the preceding 12 months 3,944. Actual number of copies of single issue published nearest to filing date 4,277. Mail subscriptions. Average number of copies each issue during preceding 12 months 22,860. Actual number of copies of single issue published nearest to filing date 25,394. C. Total paid circulation. Average number of copies each issue during preceding 12 months 26,804. Actual number of copies of single issue published nearest to filing date 29,671. D. Free distribution by mail, carrier or other means. Samples, complimentary and other free copies. Average number of copies each issue during preceding 12 months 210. Actual number of copies of single issue published nearest to filing date 219. E. Total distribution (Sum of C and D). Average number of copies each issue during preceding 12 months 27,014. Actual number of copies of single issue published nearest to filing date 29,890. F.1. Office use, leftover, unaccounted, spoiled after printing. Average number of copies each issue during preceding 12 months 1,765. Actual number of copies of single issue published nearest to filing date 1,215. 2. Returns from news agents. Average number of copies each issue during preceding 12 months 3,130. Actual number of copies of single issue published nearest to filing date 3,395. G. Total (Sum of E and F should equal net press run shown in A). Average number of copies each issue during preceding 12 months 31,909. Actual number of copies of single issue published nearest to filing date 34,500. I certify that the statements made by me above are correct and complete. Richard Rosenthal, Publisher.